(E)XTREME (H)UMAN (O)VERLOAD

DEIDRE JOHNSTON, N-D.P.G.

DIANA JOHNSON

The Henlo Press

The Henlo Press
P.O. Box 1694
Ashland, KY 41105
www.thehenlopress.com

For Midge, my sister and the pioneer in naming E.H.O. So sorry you had to do it alone until you taught us all how to love you from a distance.
—Deidre

A Letter From the Author

Hey Friend!

Do you find yourself increasingly uncomfortable in the company of those you usually hold dear? Do you find yourself making up excuses for not attending or prematurely leaving gatherings that you have planned or hosted even in your own home? Do you fantasize about jumping off a tour boat on vacation to fake your own death and assume a new identity as a vendor on a far away beach selling flip-flops and cigarettes?

Did you think you were the only poor schmuck to answer 'yes' to any of these questions?

Well I did. And it flat out made me want to run away.

Suddenly the little things I used to overlook about the people in my social circles that minimally irritated me before were now nearly impossible to endure. Every little quirk, or abrasive mannerism, or political dig, or self-absorbed behavior left me with only one thing - the urge to split!

I read all about the empty-nester adjusting to a new relationship with adult children, redefining your role with parents aging out of family involvement, and outgrowing friendships that don't serve our emotional needs. While most of the literature points to redefining these connections, it almost always suggests maintaining some semblance of the ties that bind us to one another. But what if you can't see yourself remaining connected?

As it turns out, none of the resources I referenced included the symptom I was having the worst time with, the unbridled desire to flee. I desperately searched for information that would help me justify my desire to take to my heels and leave all the familiar faces in my life in the rear view mirror, but found nothing. Now, I feel I should explain that this desire was not a destructive, world-warping hatred like you read about in the news. This was nothing like racism, bigotry, misogyny, ignorance, or fear. One day, out of the blue this immense dislike for everyone started to percolate and before I could figure out where it was coming from, it had progressed to a full-on lava flow of disdain complete with giant swelling bubbles of wanting to get the hell away from everyone! It has waxed and waned but never completely left me alone. I still struggle with exacerbations from time to time. And in its remission, I am left feeling remorseful for my actions but still strangely indifferent to the peeps in my tribe.

While I could find no supporting literature to connect this to the other changes I was experiencing with perimenopause, I was almost positive my feelings of disconnection were because of the wonderful hormonal morphing I had *enjoyed* since I began my magical journey into my middle-ages. But then I thought, *What if it isn't? What if I've just outgrown all the people I know and it's just a coincidence that it's happening now... at 52?* And I wondered if it had happened to anyone who wasn't going through "the change." Then I thought, *Man, it'd be swell if there was someone doing research on something like this!* Then I decided to pretend that *I* was. And the result is this farcical account of the discovery, research, and treatment of the malady I call Extreme Human Overload.

I cannot cure what's wrong with me right now. And rather than trying to ignore it or put on a mask of congeniality, I am choosing to embrace it and let it run its own course. However, I have found that it has less power over me when I can laugh about it. As a matter of fact, when I'm not crying in the shower, I have found some humor in it. If you or someone you love is experiencing the same thing, whether menopausal or not, I hope that by indulging in this satirical trip with me you too can attempt to get a kick out of it. Who knows, it will probably become a real thing some day and we'll all qualify for a check, a free water bottle, and a matching tote.

—The Author
Diana Johnson

What is Extreme Human Overload?

To understand the impact of any socio-psychological anomaly, one must first determine the defining parameters of normal group behavior. The human group, of course, has been examined ad nauseam by countless shamans, physicians, priests, philosophers, politicians, scientists, marketing executives, and satirists since the dawn of thinking man. We here at The Johnston and Johnston Institute For Guessing What's Wrong With People* are by no means qualified to debate the findings of these apt disciplines. We embrace their collective works and begin our explanation with the condensed result of their theories that Man is for the most part, a social animal.

If we consider the groupings of early man, we could liken the tribal configuration to that of a bull's eye.

---

* Not to be confused with Johnson & Johnson as they could not afford the "t."

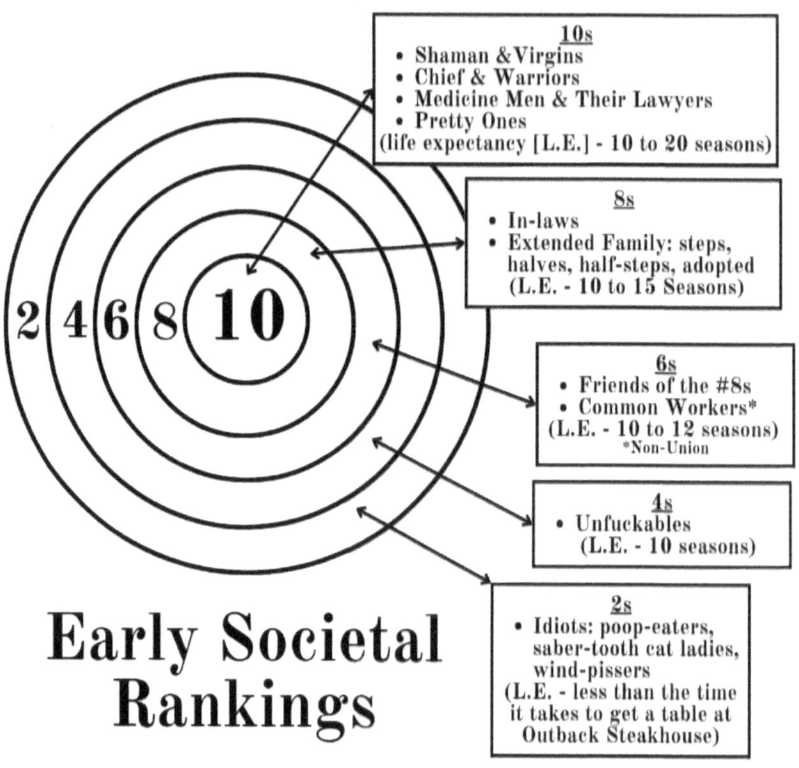

Early Society Rankings of Scientific Societal Groupings

For example, imagine the most important folks, such as: the shaman and his volcano-bate virgins, chiefs and their families, prize warriors, the medicine man and his lawyers, and the six-foot tall, ebony brunettes with sky-blue eyes, perfect teeth, and greater-than-average sized secondary sexual characteristics inhabiting the very center of this target, the 10s, if you will. This, the highest of the echelons, is the most valuable and most protected. Now the first ring around that core contains in-laws and extended family of those in the innermost circle including but not limited to grandparents, aunts and uncles, cousins, steps, halves, half-steps, and adopted stragglers. That connection gives those in the #8 ring a considerable amount of clout. Extending outwardly to ring #6, are the friends of those #8s and also common workers such as your barbers, your meat prep guys, grain mashers, and any other non-union laborers. The next ring then contains those unworthy of mating along with those with one wonky eye, nail fungus, no sense of humor, or any other undesirable trait, then idiots which includes the subclasses of poop-eaters, saber-tooth cat ladies, windwardly pissers, those unafraid of fire, and then finally the ugly people.

Now, as you might surmise, the further you are from the center of your group, the less likely you are to be cared about or protected. Indeed, we've seen evidence that some early societies didn't even know they had these outer rings per se. So if any one of the poor bastards in these lesser tiers dropped out or disappeared, little or nothing may have been done about it. But if someone originating from the innermost levels was to reject their position of inclusion in the group, this would be of great import to the rest of the folks in theirs and, probably, the immediate lesser levels. While this has not been the "norm" for folks seemingly comfortable and cared for, it *has* occurred. Actions like these have been recorded in almost every society since we've been keeping tabs on ourselves and with that as evidence, we began to identify the beginnings of this phenomenon, Extreme Human Overload.

In mankind's earliest days together, acting on the urge to separate yourself from your group had grave consequences. Those left unprotected by their peers were eaten by predators, captured by rival tribes, or succumbed to the ravages of nature. These people took a colossal risk rejecting their positions and withdrawing from their assemblage. But if they were indeed suffering (as we think they were) from primitive E.H.O., they may have felt as if they had no choice but to bolt. Those suffering from this disorder have been reported as being possessed by an undeniable urge to flee from the safety of their group no matter the results. They are overwhelmed with the same faces and opinions of familiar family, friends, and coworkers and just can't stand to be around them anymore. All things being relative, our ancestors, safe within the protection of their groups or not, probably survived as long as our present-day wait-for-a-table-at-the-local-steakhouse-on-a-Friday-night-without-call-ahead-seating. However, their individual lives and how they fit into and dropped out of their communities is mirrored in our own current culture.

In present day society, we've witnessed folks from Royal families, rock bands, major corporations, and the like turn their backs to the comforts and privilege their lives have afforded them only to disappear into obscurity with no more of a threat than being cut off from their great-granddaddy's fortune. These individuals may have been experiencing an overwhelming of sorts, simply unable to manage while still remaining within their given group. And in today's culture of currency worship, it serves as a kind of litmus test that when the average Joe can't figure out why in hell a super-rich, well connected, gorgeous, well received, set-for-life douchebag announces that he's quitting the family, you can bet your sweet bippy it's the beginnings of Extreme Human Overload. While these high-profile cases are most prominent, it can happen to any of us regardless of financial security, social status, cultural practices, or intellect. With the population of the world nearing 8 billion, we predict that by 2026, 4.83 billion (or approximately 61% for you math nerds out there) of folks will tire of their people and disassociate from their original groups.

By understanding this syndrome and treating those affected while also educating those in their support systems, we hope to be able to keep our social threads from unraveling further. Our lives have been manipulated toward separation for centuries by the powers that profit so they can successfully divide and conquer us. Extreme Human Overload may be a direct, trickle-down effect of these powerful pressures. When one becomes exhausted by the members of one's group, one can simply depart without notice or explanation. This is certainly not the way our species was designed to behave, and we here at The Institute are determined to reunite the excused with his set.

Now that we've generally explained E.H.O., let's look at some specifics of the disorder. We hope to unlock the mysteries of this syndrome so that all who read this introductory volume may benefit.

E.H.O. is a syndrome of diverse symptoms that manifest in innumerable ways. Table 1 identifies some signs and symptoms reported from sufferers and the girls in their group. This is not a complete listing as research is ongoing.

Sample of Symptoms - Table 1

Clinical Symptom	Average Manifestation
Reduction in Overall Communication	Diminished answered calls, emails, texts or Facebook posts, or no returned messages at all.
Communication Cut Short	Any abrupt cessation of communication: the hang-up, the "your brea-ing u-," and the ever-concerning, albeit irritating, "I'm done!"
Change in General Communication	Changing voicemail messages from something cute and personal to the pre-recorded, robotic version that came with the phone. Or in advanced cases, a *truthful* message including phrases like "I don't want to talk to you" or "Piss Off!"
Changes in Appearance	Any significant weight loss could signify them taking more time for themselves and thus creating improved health (again irritating). Significant weight gain may indicate the early stages of reclusive behavior that inevitably ends in big machinery taking your house apart to get your dead body out for the funeral a.k.a. public gawking.
Venomous Speech	Any hateful rhetoric usually reserved for discussions of child molesters and rapists being employed when speaking about such things as the Mother-Daughter covered dish dinner at your neighbor's church, i.e. *'Dixie's up to her felonious shit again, trying to pass that potato salad off as her own. Someone needs to cut that bitch!'*
Disconnecting From All Groups	Reports from friends, utilities, and reunion committees that you or your loved one has simply, "dropped off the radar."

The symptoms of Extreme Human Overload should not be confused with premenstrual syndrome, situational or chronic depression, the beginnings of deterioration in a failing marriage, empty-nest syndrome, postpartum baby blues, puberty, or midlife crises. And make no mistake, E.H.O. can and often does occur concurrently with the above mentioned as well as many other interruptions in mental balance. It can, and often does manifest after the acute phase of these and other maladies have passed as well. It can be the result of "too damned much attention to self." For instance, E.H.O. may occur following a long, troubled pregnancy and complicated delivery of a child, or after multiple attempts by your friends to fix you up with every single, female animal within a hundred miles following an ugly divorce. These more common types of life's hiccups are usually transient and manageable with medication, talk therapy, or family support. However, signs of E.H.O. have also been documented in those showing no apparent struggle with any other disorder, only adding to its mystery. Those with a stand-alone diagnosis of E.H.O. exclude themselves for fuck's sake and leave the rest of us helpless in our efforts to understand or aid them.

Unlike the other disorders referenced above, the symptoms of Extreme Human Overload are felt deep in the psyche and often leave abysmal trenches of abhorrence and odium in their wake. Ultimately, more tragic than the damage is the inability for anyone to reach these people who have as the signature action of the syndrome suggests, shit-canned the group! But hope should not be abandoned as there are many classes of E.H.O. and although recovery from each offers specific challenges, they are all treatable.

Class I – Sufferers of this class may only be beginning to show symptoms of irritation with those in their circle. Friends may see this person bowing out of the ritualistic Sunday dinner at Gammy and Pops'. They may commit to lunch with friends only to cancel at the last minute or fake an emergency just as you get your menus and hurry away. The clue for connecting this type of sit-and-run behavior to the syndrome is of course, no apology. If someone must cut an engagement short or miss one altogether and they say, *"I'm so sorry, but I left my puppy on the stove… I really have to go!"* this person probably does NOT have Extreme Human Overload. However, if the scenario is one such as, "Hup… that's me. Can't stay," you can be sure E.H.O. is beginning to creep in. Lack of reasonable remorse is one of the signature characteristics we find in all Overloaders. If you're sorry when you've been a jackass, you're not too far gone. If the syndrome is missed and treatment is not initiated at this early level, symptoms will most definitely worsen.*

Class II – This level of illness includes a subclass of the afflicted known as the Perpetually Repellent Ignorant Chowderhead Know-it-all, or P.R.I.C.K., to be brief. P.R.I.C.K.s can seemingly come out of nowhere (acute onset) or their acidity can be so pervasive that they go virtually unnoticed in their clique (the chronic P.R.I.C.K.). A P.R.I.C.K. will insist on the group coming to them instead of visiting anyone else's home. This affords them the sovereignty to challenge or veto any behavior they find irritating while still *appearing* to be interested in inclusion. A P.R.I.C.K. will keep his television tuned to Fox News if he knows a moderate, liberal, or even a social-republican will visit. He may even mute the volume completely, to again appear hospitable, when he knows that even just reading the ticker of *breaking news* along the bottom of the screen is enough to drive any reasonably thinking person to hysteria. P.R.I.C.K.s have been known to direct racist, misogynistic, and otherwise disrespectful comments pointedly to the children in the room, for instance, referencing Dora The Explorer as "that obnoxious little brown bitch" who "better have Swiper swipe her a visa or we're going to deport her back to El Me-hi-co." †

Unlike those suffering from Class I E.H.O., in an effort to separate

---

* It is important to note that even if the victim deteriorates to the worst case, treatment can still be successful, but in recovery, one may revisit lesser classes on their way to wellness. So, progressing from this class to the next and even the next and *then* initiating treatment does not guarantee one will not regress to Class I and again be regarded as "Cousin Asshole." Another fact worth noting is that recovery from Class I is much less painful and requires less time and/or rehabilitating handicrafts to achieve than the more intense Classes II and III.

† The Johnston & Johnston Institute For Guessing What's Wrong With People in no way condones racism of any kind either toward actual or animated persons, nor do we support ANY contemporary policy on immigration. Why can't we figure this one out? Just sayin'.

themself from the pack, the P.R.I.C.K. attempts to drive everyone around them away. So it appears that their circle has left *them* and not the other way around. P.R.I.C.K.s are the absolute hardest to reach for recovery. You may know if you have ever tried to reason with a P.R.I.C.K., they are set in their ways and usually require repeated interventions if they are to be helped at all. Any attempt to convince a P.R.I.C.K. that their actions are antisocial are usually met with such classic rhetoric as, "If you don't like it, get the hell out!" and the ever frustrating, "Who the hell said I wanted to be 'social' anyway?" And finally, unlike the Class III casualties, P.R.I.C.K.s are rarely self-destructive. Some P.R.I.C.K.s have been known to outlive all their immediate relations and most of their friends, if they ever had any. Rarely are these folks convinced to seek treatment before they've driven everyone who would care to see them recover right out of their lives. For this reason, Class II Extreme Human Overload research has somewhat dead ended. Teams at The Institute are consistently reaching out to study these people, but the P.R.I.C.K.s keep pissing them off. We have lost many talented lab assistants who just simply couldn't remain objective enough to continue to study them.

Class III – Finally we examine the third and most intense class of Extreme Human Overload. Even though those suffering from Class II are less likely to become rehabilitated, the Class III client is much more likely to self-destruct. For this reason, this class of E.H.O. is referred to as the "terminal" class. Please again keep in mind that treatment has been initiated in this class with some measure of success, but most often Class III Overloaders go on to "meet Jesus*" as a result of their disorder. Inherent in this classification is a continuum along which victims can be found sometimes as seemingly polar opposites. Nonetheless, anyone belonging to this third class will

---

* If you find yourself offended by this colloquialism, feel free to insert another from the following list that better suits your sensitivities; go west, kick the bucket, pop one's clogs, push up daisies, sleep with the fishes, croak, join the church triumphant, take a dirt nap, succumb to the pantod, cross the bar, give up the ghost, bite the dust, buy the farm.

possess at least some of the identifying criteria. To fully understand all subclasses in this level of disease, we must imagine a combination of the Class I Asshole and the Class II P.R.I.C.K. And this is only the beginning of the Class III profile. Add to these fundamental personality types the wealth and power necessary to manipulate whole sections of the population, or the poverty and humility to live and work around the people most unlikely to survive and you have a Class III diagnosis of Extreme Human Overload.The historic cases of this class were not satisfied with voluntarily withdrawing from their assemblage, nor were they content with driving the others around them away. Class III Overloaders have targeted whole races and classes of people around them for systematic annihilation in an effort to customize the company they keep. These are pathologically BIG thinkers who spend hundreds of thousands of hours over a lifetime conjuring up ways in which to distance themselves from certain people in their lot. And on the other end of the continuum, there are those who choose a life of service to a population most likely to be wiped out by one of their comrades in this third class. These poor sons-a-bitches will appear to strive to save nearly everyone around them, knowing full well that they'll be alone soon and look the part of the martyr in doing so. The majority of Class III subjects to have been studied were examined posthumously by reviewing public records and interviewing the survivors of their attempts to express their E.H.O. Some of the better known victims of Class III have been thought to possess 'evil genius'. Others have been referred to as 'saints*' This category of the syndrome, though diverse in its participants, almost always ends in the actions of the victim either directly or indirectly facilitating their own death. We explore in greater detail examples of Class III disease in Chapter 3, Some Famous Cases.

---

* As listed in The Dictionary of This, That, and What Have You; evil genius - synonyms: Charles and/or David Koch, The Boogie Man, Richard Bruce Cheney, and according to some accounts Mary Kate and Ashley Olsen [see also Evil Twin].

Saints - synonyms: Val Kilmer, Deuce McAllister, anyone found to have gone 'marching in', and Mary, Joe's wife.

Now that we have defined Extreme Human Overload in its most basic forms, let's move forward to examine who among us may be at risk.

$$\overline{}$$

2

Who is at Risk for E.H.O.?

$$\overline{}$$

WHEN STUDYING the specific population affected by a newly defined condition, science and medicine begin comparing what all the subjects share in common. This was the tactic employed when we discovered Extreme Human Overload— a task that seemed nearly impossible, as our test groups were so incredibly diverse. We interviewed housewives, retired service personnel, clergymen, members of both the House and Senate, contractors, artists, refs and umpires, Little Caesars Pizza-Pizza sign dancers, mall Santas, rug hookers, rugby hookers, plain ole hookers, fifth grade bullies, Chihuahua groomers, meter maids, life guards from Senior Swim, notary publics, and a cast of others all exhibiting signs and symptoms with absolutely no common threads connecting them outside of those signs and symptoms.

This syndrome is so prolific it can infiltrate the most secure sects of society and sometimes without warning, pluck out those seemingly embedded in their pack. It should be noted that some cases studied to date did show many warning signs that were too subtle or cloaked to raise an eyebrow from those surrounding the individual.

So, who is at risk for E.H.O.? Just about everyone on the planet.

E.H.O. can infiltrate the most secure sects of our society and sometimes without warning. No one is safe from E.H.O.

With such diverse symptoms and the risk of concurrent diagnoses, the face of Extreme Human Overload takes on an "every man" profile. Certainly, the majority of confirmed cases are in the adult community, but our research is documenting more and more pediatric patients. If your child exhibits the traits of what old wives have historically referred to as an *old soul,* they may be predisposed to E.H.O. Having acquired greater than age-appropriate wisdom and maturity can signal fully living a parallel life, reincarnation from a past one, or other such silly shit that could happen between planes of existence. With this "otherness" there could be pre-existing loathing of the troop. If a child appears to be a loner, spending hours alone to the discomfort of family and friends, assessment for E.H.O. may be warranted. However, a quiet child is sometimes just introspective and treatment for Overload is like CPR, if the victim doesn't need it, it could hurt 'em! So care must be taken with assessment and diagnosis to avoid such harm. Many a child has been worried into a pseudo state of the disease by anxious parents or overzealous clinicians looking for journal publication opportunities.

One of our youngest test subjects was Baby A who at 6 weeks of age was already signaling to her mother that she didn't want to be around anyone she'd met so far. This infant, perfectly healthy in every other way, cried only when she was being held. She grunted rudely when being changed or fed as if she understood those things *had* to be done for her own daily care, and as she was unable to do for herself, she reluctantly submitted to those care measures. However, when she was clean and fed, if she was not afforded privacy in her layette or crib, she would wail as if being dipped in hot wax. Baby A would have to be considered a congenital case of the Class II variety, as there was little or nothing in the early days of this child's life to nurture this response to others. Although it should be noted that as we tracked her and her family up until the time of this writing, both her father and her mother (divorced now and re-coupled with others) have and do exhibit some signs of suffering from E.H.O. Her older brother had a brief period of Class II symptoms erupt around his senior year in high school, but was never diagnosed as it has been our conclusion that just about every boy that age behaves as a P.R.I.C.K. for a short burst. With the subsequent family involvement though, new questions arise as to the possibility of either hereditary or contagious E.H.O.

Next we should examine the involvement of hormone fluctuation amid the Overloaders. This variable can challenge two groups of individuals: the teen and the menopausal. The teen, having just arrived in a place in social development where they expect and indeed need to identify with a new group, can almost immediately upon inclusion in that group, develop Extreme Human Overload. These individuals will first pull away from family, appearing to take the rite of passage into young adulthood without the safety net of their inherited tribe. But then, upon closer examination of the new peer congregation, they can again inexplicably bow out. In clinical testing, our subject Mr. Q, a 15-year-old male, attempted to categorize himself as a loner. He exhibited romantic ideals of a James Dean type exile. When we probed for more historical information, we learned that as soon as he started shaving (around 12.5 years of age), he no longer kissed his mother in public, avoided being seen with his little sister, and refused to let his father tussle his hair or call him "little man." These indeed were the initial red flags to signal the onset of E.H.O. However, and adding to the difficulty of diagnosis and treatment of this mysterious syndrome, these could also be normal developments in the teenage psyche. It was only on further examination that our team was able to uncover that this young man in particular, had yet another layer of societal withdrawal.

After many sessions of testing and therapeutic activities including, but not limited to, designing and sewing clothes for pets, this subject related that he desired to take leave of his new peer group as well. He had taken up with a collection of Goths and math nerds who called themselves the Gomaterds. They were an assemblage of dismally intelligent youths with a propensity toward writing and submitting fake cryptic obituaries in which trigonometry and hieroglyphics were employed to lead people on fictitious quests for hidden treasures in the private back yards of citizens in the community who were still very much alive. Our subject related that he couldn't relate. Mr. Q's case was, unlike the transient case of Baby A's big brother, Class I and very much treatable. With the help of the professionals at The Institute and his natural occurring hormonal peak, this subject returned to his nuclear family, graduated from a second-rate college, and even became a prominent member of several ineffectual fraternal organizations. It should be noted that much to the chagrin of his mother, his symptoms did not fully subside until some time after his 25th birthday, and the coincidental complete development of his prefrontal cortex*.

Here we must also include some specificity that can be present in

---

* We learned about this in an All State commercial.

the female teen, illuminating some fundamental differences between our male and female clients. Unfortunately, our lab technicians repeatedly had much abbreviated sessions with most of our female teenage subjects. When a female teen exhibits symptoms of Extreme Human Overload there is a lot of hysterical crying and screaming phrases like, "I hate you!", "You're ruining my life!", and "Your new wife has a thicker mustache than my soccer coach!" followed by their forcefully exiting the room. For this reason, and apologetically so, we quit working with teenage girls altogether. We did unequivocally conclude that no one can stand to be around these bitches and so this certainly would make for the beginnings of E.H.O, Class II.

Again with hormonal changes in mind, we direct our attention to the menopausal woman who represents a staggering 92.34% of cases studied to date. Begging the question, is it all because of menopause? These subjects of our research were most dear to me because of my own family history of E.H.O. and the losses associated with it. I was determined to isolate the origins of the problem and give it hell! The menopausal woman, as illustrated by our Ms. D, can be, and often is, a productive and prominent figure in both her own family grouping and those of her friends and coworkers. She can exhibit no warning signs and then seemingly out of nowhere, once her estrogen and progesterone levels begin to fluctuate, present with the worst case of acute onset Overload. Ms. D was a middle aged wife and mother who, having tried a couple of times at marriage with the wrong sort of fellow, had finally arrived in a respectful and loving relationship. She was successfully rearing her daughter after having had sons with a semi-professional curler from Sweden to practice on in her twenties* and making her way professionally teaching anatomy in a small private massage therapy school. Her family had just purchased a new home, a modest ranch on a small private lot with a swimming pool. Everyone in Ms. D's life, including Ms. D, was elated that she finally arrived at a place in life where she could relax and enjoy her bad self.

---

* Making colossal mistakes with children is documented as one of the leading causes of middle-aged women developing E.H.O.

The new house was company friendly with an inviting back porch leading to the wet and wonderful poolside. Ms. D moved into her new home at the end of June and the outside space was readied for summer fun. After that initial summer of entertaining a different group of friends or family every *bloody* weekend, Ms. D's behavior began to become bitter and biting. She was aggressive and confrontational with her husband. She was short with her daughter. And soon she began avoiding correspondence with everyone. She skipped family functions, lied about the pool being worked on to ward off any drop-ins to swim, and she spent more and more time crying in her room following venomous, emotional outbursts.

In an attempt to understand her own behavioral issues, she sought out the wisdom of her older sister, with whom she hadn't spoken but for a few obligatory catch-up calls since she began feeling this way. Her sister reportedly listened intently and told her in a reassuring tone that she was suffering from what she called the E.H.O. or Extreme Human Overload*. This subject and her sister were paramount to our research and their story will be examined in depth in a later chapter, as they are textbook versions of how hormones can be the catalyst for an onset of Extreme Human Overload.

Another grouping of Overloaders worth singling out here is the retiree, a.k.a. grumpy old man. While a rise in testosterone can be blamed for the young man's descent into E.H.O. a decline in the level of that same hormone has been clinically connected to the onset of the syndrome among retired men. Without their genitals directing their lives, many older men begin to withdraw from or change the company within their social groups. A man who was previously active in a professional fraternity or union may slowly begin receding from the activities of those cliques. When those types of social groups meet in establishments that offer alcoholic beverages served by even semi-attractive female employees as little as 10 to 20 years their juniors, the

---

* Ms. D was indeed in the throes of Class II disease and it was later determined through Ancestry.com that her grandmother as well had been and remained until the time of her death, a Class II P.R.I.C.K.; again pointing our research toward the hereditary nature of this erosive disease.

retired gentlemen showing the initial signs of E.H.O. will begin making random excuses for not attending the events. Since most men equate their own sexual virility with their place in this world, it is no secret that many who reach the age of retirement and who are among the normal population of fellows having a reduced blood testosterone level and thus a decreased libido, want to vacate their spot on the team.

Interestingly, with this group of subjects, there is often a feigned attempt at appearing unaffected by these physiological and psychosocial changes. Mr. P was a masculine man who had a masculine job all of his productive masculine years. He stayed in top physical condition and was considered by his own account to be quite the ladies' man. When he retired from his career and began experiencing the occasional "misfire" while engaged with a woman, Mr. P began feeling awkward and odd when socializing with his peers. His confidence shaken, what would normally be a raucous night at the lodge with the guys, flirting with the waitresses just up to the point but not crossing over into criminal assault, became a painful exercise in how not to appear as an impotent, dried-out, old fart. These men can feel an extreme amount of pretend pressure on them to be the life of the party even after all the "party" has left their masculine lives. In an attempt to cover up his insecurities, Mr. P began overacting the part of the ladies' man, often to the point of becoming even more obnoxious and off-putting than before. It wasn't until a friend of his (a gent recovering from Extreme Human Overload himself) spotted Mr. P's over-the-top public displays alternated with his underlying discomfort and recognized his occasional absences as familiar symptoms. Through careful examination of his issues and hours of constructing enough tissue paper carnations to cover a float in the Rose Bowl Parade, Mr. P was welcomed back into the fold. Peer support in this case enabled the subject to take the first steps toward diagnosis and treatment. This element and others will be visited in the chapters on Viable Treatments and Support for Overloaders.

While our anonymous clinical subjects shed general light on E.H.O. and who may be at risk, like so many other maladies discovered in the history of recorded medicine, no examples are more interesting or educational than famous people who suffer. So in the next chapter we examine high profile cases of Extreme Human Overload.

3

Some Famous Cases of (E)xtreme (H)uman (O)verload.

WHEN WE EXAMINE *celebrity* (pardon the italics but I hope to emphasize this term as a pronoun), we can witness a plethora of behaviors that could either mimic or signal the onset of Extreme Human Overload. Examples of some of these include firing your agent, moving to another country, quitting the band to be with your artist girlfriend, walking out in the middle of your own circumcision, photo shoot, interview, wedding, haircut, child's birth, dental cleaning, dissertation, deposition, or just generally becoming scarce. And while living life in the public eye may not be for everyone, most who try for fame usually accept the bother of it along with the glamor. There have been more than a few famous folks, though, who've given up the glitz and retreated as far out of the spotlight as they could get.

Bumpass Bulletin

INSTITUTE UNCOVERS SHOCKING NEW CELEBRITY CASE OF E.H.O.

The new diagnosis sweeping the nation– Is no one safe from the spectacular syndrome?

Researchers at The Johnston & Johnston Institute for Guessing What's Wrong with People disclosed in a press conference yesterday that they have posthumously diagnosed yet another celebrity with the illusive disorder of Extreme Human Overload. Until permissions can be obtained from the victim's next of kin, The institute cannot reveal the name of the celebrity in question, but sources close to this reporter say he was male, of rural American descent, he had a twin who died, he was obsessive/compulsive about his blue suede shoes, and that none of his friends were hound dogs. The press began wildly speculating about his identity, but the researchers refused to confirm or deny any guesses as they had not secured the proper consents to reveal his identity.

Learn More About the Institute and What They Do For Our Community

Does your pet need a status boost?

You can't have the other dogs at the dog park looking down on your best friend now, can you? Put that pooch in a custom suit or gown made especially for your furry friend by the patients at The Johnston &Johnston Institute for Guessing What's Wrong with People. Bring your pet in to be measured and choose from hundreds of dress and casual styles

TO CONTINUE READING IN FASHION, TURN TO PAGE 6.

Local Bumpass, VA newspaper clipping speculating on celeb E.H.O. cases.

We need to establish the difference here between true syndrome sufferers and those simply ill-equipped to deal with life in the limelight. Those like Bobby Fisher who buckled under the pressures of performance and threw shit-hissy fits to the point of getting kicked out of the country, may have been attempting to distance themselves from their peer group (namely those cheating Soviet bastards!). But then again, he may have just lacked the coping skills of someone more mature or better grounded. And someone like Stanley Kubrick, who may only appear to be reclusive, may just prefer to stay on his own side of The Pond.

Then there are your Dave Chappelles, your Johnny Depps, your Lauren Hills. These people either cracked up, fucked up, or got fed up. They dropped out, or ducked out, or just laid low until they felt like taking a shot at public life again. They all returned to some degree from their self-exile. These folks probably did not suffer from E.H.O., at least not in the full blown "syndromey" sense of the disease. I mean every celebrity probably gets tired of the lack of privacy, but Bill Watterson and Steve Ditko for chrissake? No one even knows what they look like*.

If you ask any mainstream inhabitant of these United States to name a famous person who left that mainstream to live a secluded life, your top three contestants are probably Howard Hughes, J.D. Salinger, and Earnest Hemingway. These are America's superstars of Extreme Human Overload. The creative mind is a playground for emotional havoc, and these three are certainly seen as creative if nothing else. We choose here to match up Jerry and Ernie for comparison. As contemporaries even though they were born 20 years apart, they communicated with one another, they both wrote short stories and novels, served their country, were born and died in the same months (Salinger was a New Year's baby and died January 27 & Hemingway entered July 21 and exited July 2–our research guys insist on me including this trivial shit!). Seemingly similar in these ways, their E.H.O. presented differently.

Salinger, obviously a Class I clear up until his death in 2010, he

---

* Note to Bill and Steve… Come on you guys, just avoid the crowds at Comic-Con and you could probably live out the rest of your days without even so much as a telemarketer bothering you. P.S. We'd love to get one of *you* two in the lab.

often displayed what was misinterpreted as rude and cranky behavior, when we can speculate now that he was suffering from this socially misunderstood disease. Hemingway, we conclude, was in the grips of Class II symptoms but may have prematurely jumped ahead to the final stages of Class III, as he opted out early through booze and suicide.

This brings us to Mr. Hughes. Howard Robard Hughes, Jr.

Sure, he was an eccentric teenage billionaire. Sure, he never graduated high school. Sure, he was obsessive compulsive. Sure, he was a hypochondriac. Sure, he was involved in spy rings, assassination plots, hostile corporate takeovers, and wild sexual romps with Hollywood actresses. Sure, he was a relentless perfectionist. This guy makes the Kardashian-Jenners look like June and Ward Cleaver, one hot mess to be sure. But did all these other behaviors simply point to the all-inclusive Extreme Human Overload?

His Uncle Rupert tried to guide him along after his folks departed and enabled him to get a leg up with the Hughes Tool Company. One can speculate that an operation as substantial and profitable would either be an incredible opportunity for the young Hughes or a giant cock-up waiting to happen. But as history and famoustexans.com would show us, Howard did well in spurts with all his financial endeavors, buying airlines, movie studios, state secrets, presidents, and such proved lucrative biz, to say the least. What thrilling days and nights this young man must have spent with all those actresses, transportation moguls, and politicians. However, this kind of instant financial responsibility and notoriety can overcome an individual to the point of developing craziness of the bat-shit variety. His constant state of flux, dictating his abrupt change of focus from one project to another was definitely Class I material. He could avoid problems with people in the movie industry by jumping ship midstream and diving into deals with TWA at the drop of a hat. Even though he kept a small handful of steadfast anchors employed over the majority of his life, he hired and fired at will, frequently changing the personnel landscape around him. We can also recognize Class II symptoms when examining his personal connections.

His psychological autopsy, performed by American Psychological Association's Raymond D. Fowler, PhD, concluded that his correspondence and associates' recollections "painted a picture... of a young child who pretty much was isolated and had no friends..." So we are posthumously lumping Junior into concurrent diagnoses of Class I and II. And now we direct our attention away from our home shores to the world at large. For the next two cases, we must explore the continuum on which Class III victims can be found. As introduced in Chapter 1, the range of symptoms, personality traits, and behaviors can be wide indeed in Class III. Although one trait prevails all along the continuum and that is that whole sects of the victim's common citizenry are precariously poised for destruction. So to create a framework from which to categorize these individuals, we have chosen to borrow the example our fellows in the mathematical sciences employ with their rational and irrational numbers (We really don't understand anything about these mathematical terms but we liked the way they described our subjects so we felt we had to throw out a holla!). We have chosen to place dastardly villains at the irrational end of the continuum and loving humanitarians at the rational end.

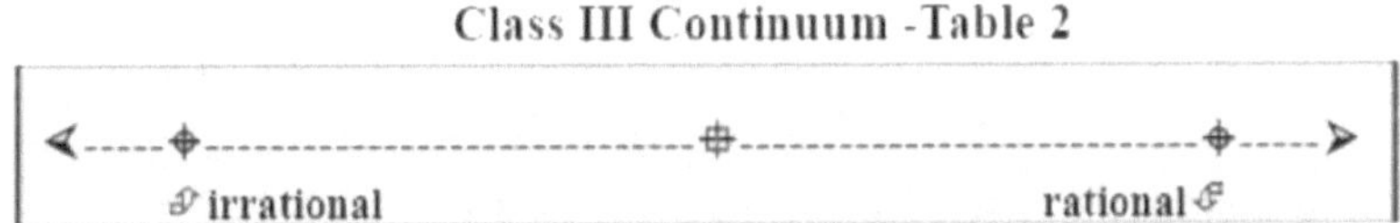

The official scale of the Class III Irrational/Rational Range.

Irrational End of the Continuum - Few names in recent history project a more beastly picture in our imaginations than Adolph Hitler's. This mad man and the atrocities he inflicted on millions of people have been the subject of numerous investigations and examinations. We shudder to think of what the world would be like today if he had been successful in continuing his campaign throughout Europe and eventually the rest of the world. Let's face it, at the very least, Hollywood would just be the pimento in the olive of L.A. and you could expire looking for a good bagel. And while thousands of other physicians, scientists, historians, and my dad have studied his evil genius, Hitler has been one of the most prominent "famous case studies" of our own institution as well. He had such a pronounced case of Class III disease that he amassed an army to rid the world, not just his surrounding neighborhood, but the WORLD of the Jewish population. And this little parlor trick was only one phase of his grand plan. When we first discussed naming this syndrome, it was Adolph Hitler's example that directed us toward the "Extreme" in Extreme Human Overload. On the continuum of the Class III disease, Mr. Hitler* is at the most extreme, irrational end. His heinous crimes against humanity were his attempt to shrink the population and thus limit his contact with a number of extra people. As we all know, his fate was sealed with his own suicide in keeping with the usual outcome of this, the terminal class of E.H.O.

Hitler began to show signs of being a Class I Asshole at age 11 following his brother Edmund's death to measles. A rift between him and his father that would never be mended contributed to his graduation to P.R.I.C.K status in his early teens. Following his father's untimely death when young Adolph was only 14 years of age, he made haste to distance himself from his family and seek out the anonymity of the streets of Vienna. As he had been expelled from several schools and fancied himself an artist, he tried the bohemian lifestyle for as long as he could without starving. Rejected by The Academy of Fine Arts *twice*, what began as a bratty pout, quickly became his slow descent into madness and the rest is history. And with all the evil in

---

* Man, I hate even eking out enough respect for this monster to refer to him as "Mr.", so I'll use his native language to dub him kranker Scheiß - which loosely translated, means 'sick fuck' in English.

this world before and since, we at The Institute are of the collective opinion that *this* kranker Scheiß takes the cake! Even with just an elementary understanding of E.H.O. one could easily understand placing this subject at the not-nice end of the continuum. And knowing that it seems that the other end of this range couldn't be far enough away from any other soul to make a case for them, we humbly ask you for your longest stretch of tolerance and imagination while we present the next case.

Rational End of the Continuum – As repelling as the last subject was, our example of this end of the continuum is just as endearing. Mother Teresa of Calcutta, a name synonymous with love and charity, also suffered from Class III Extreme Human Overload. I know, you're asking yourself, "Are they fucking kidding me right now? Adolph and Terri on the same continuum?" And no, we are dead-fucking-serious. Mother Teresa's story begins 21 years after the furor's birth in Albania, part of the "Ottoman" on which Austria-Hungary rested her feet (intentional pun for those kooky geography buffs out there). She too lost her father early in life. She was only eight when he passed. Her mother's hard work, faith, and prayers sustained the family, but Anjeze(Agnes) Gonxhe Bojaxhiu (yes, that was her given name) went all the way to Ireland ten years later to join the Sisters of Loreto. Not only had she fled her nuclear family and her country of origin, which is classic Class I behavior, she changed her name! Now she was to be called Sister Mary Teresa after St. Therese of Lisieux a.k.a. The Little Flower*.

In the year 1931, Mother Teresa again fled her new peers and relocated to Calcutta, India. It was here that she began teaching at the St. Mary's School for Girls, becoming principal in 1944. From this move, one could surmise that she may have overcome her Class I symptoms

---

* Incidentally, St. Therese may also have suffered from Class III disease as she was only fifteen when she joined the Carmelite order at Lisieux and caught TB and died by the age of twenty-four. Mother Teresa's self-destruction, unlike that of her namesake, was less noticeable, taking eight decades and then some.

and found a group in which she comfortably fit. But just two years later on a train ride from Darjeeling, she reportedly experienced a "calling within a calling" and went off in another direction yet again. This time, experts tell us that after several long and drawn out discussions with Jesus himself, she was bent on finding him more "victims of love," Upon her return she quickly left the school and began roaming the streets of Calcutta, *her* bohemian phase if you will. We think she was attempting to blend in to the masses thus cloaking herself from all her previous groups. She ministered to the sick and dying. She fed the hungry and housed the poor. The poor, sick, hungry, and dying, these were not robust groups. She knew that none of these poor saps would make it. She deliberately chose these "victims" as Jesus had so aptly put it on the train, to commune with in an effort to one day be without a group again.

On this side of the E.H.O. Class III coin, opposite all the death and despair, pain and havoc to be wreaked by Hitler, is the love and charity, compassion and peace multiplied by Mother Teresa. Her suffering from the most deadly class of the syndrome afforded millions of lost souls heavenly comfort on their journey from this life. And for this effort, we here at The Institute salute our most compassionate and selfless subject, thank you, Mother Teresa! We only regret that our facility wasn't founded until 2003, a full 6 years after her demise. Would that we could have administered treatment to this beautiful soul, she may still be with us... but really old*.

---

* Seeing as how all of the folks in this chapter have either never been officially assessed, diagnosed, or even lived during our speculation of their apparent suffering of Extreme Human Overload, we ask that you keep this information to yourself as we cannot afford any more liable suits at The Johnston & Johnston Institute For Guessing What's Wrong With People. Thank you.

4

The Research

As you may imagine, guessing what's wrong with people is an arduous task on a good day. And we here at The Institute have left no stone unturned as we endeavor to amass the greatest body of research into the tragic syndrome of Extreme Human Overload. We chose to model our research in an integrative fashion instead of creating a linear path that would not allow for the diversity of our subjects or the many facets of the syndrome itself. This itself proved to be daunting because let's face it, at least with a line you have some direction to follow. We were convinced that were we to mimic the linear examples in similar fields of research that we may find ourselves missing many key elements that could prove to be instrumental in our study.

As is the trend with quantitative studies, the team assigned to gather facts about E.H.O. began with questions, namely: Why do these individuals abandon their groups? And, is there a way to get them to rejoin? So with these questions to guide us, we began.

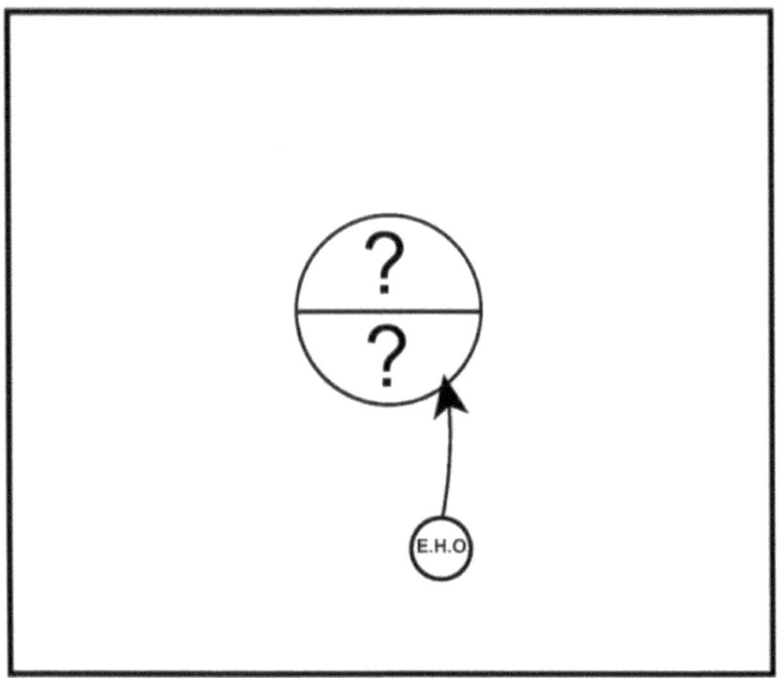

Instititue Assessment Tool: Step One

Next we chose the goals we hoped to accomplish with our research, namely: creating a 5-Step Assessment Tool to diagnose and a 5-Phase Treatment Protocol to treat E.H.O. So, with these goals to steer our project we continued.

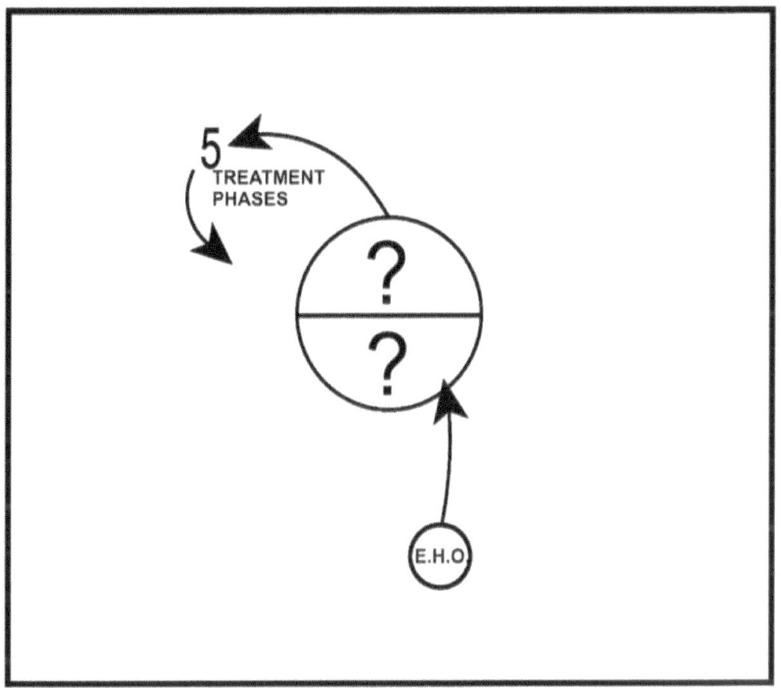

Instititue Assessment Tool: Step Two

Then, we constructed the conceptual framework from which to work. As a group, we theorized four concepts: 1) that all humans want and need to belong to a social group; 2) sometimes people drop out; 3) this must be a deviation from the norm; and 4) that people need to be returned to the safety of their group. So, with these concepts on which we agreed, our research progressed.

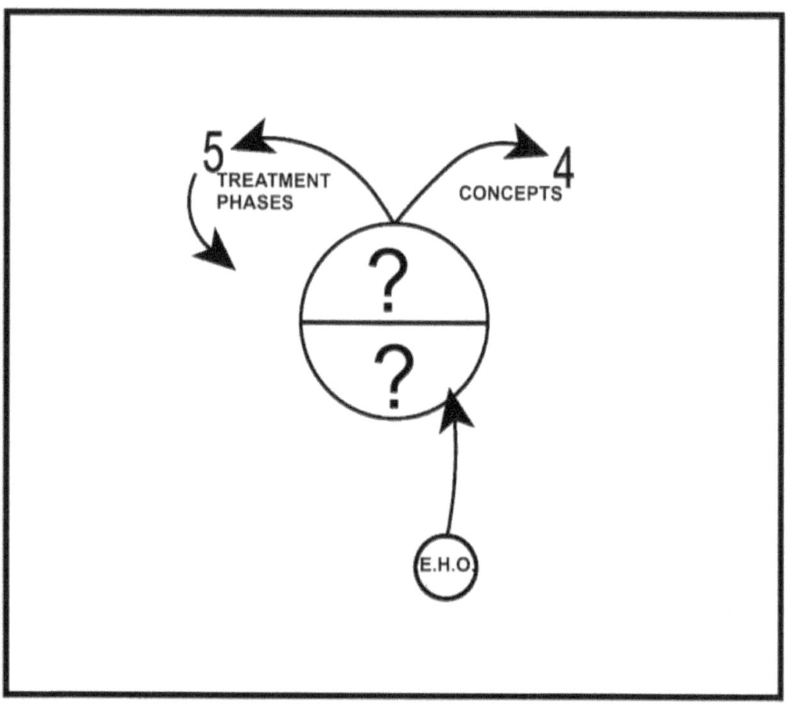

Instititue Assessment Tool: Step Three

It was then that we developed the three distinct methods we would employ to achieve the outcomes of our research.

- First, of course, we would engage control and focus groups in guided and open group sessions.
- Second, we would approach singular subjects to observe both in private sessions and when permitted in everyday activities.
- Third, we would use a great many paper and computerized questionnaires.

So, with our methods prepared we soldiered on.

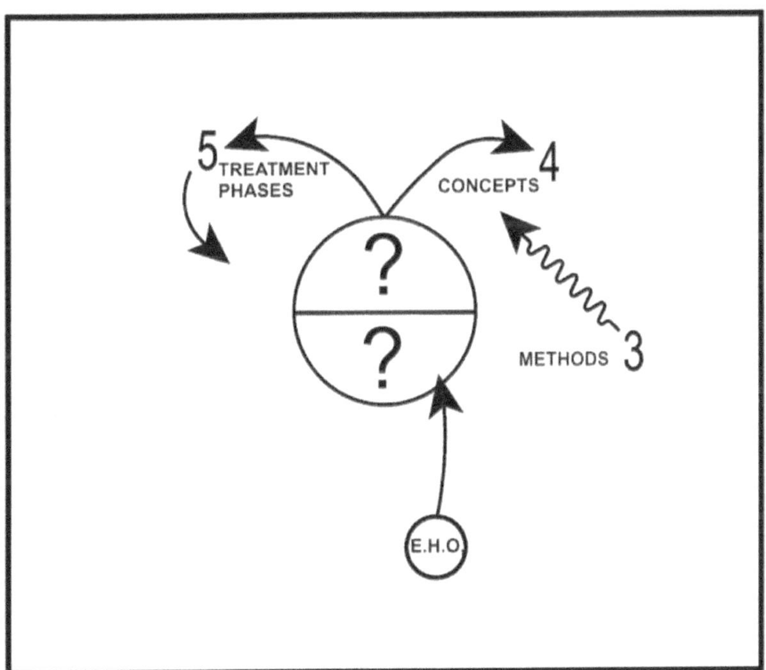

Instititue Assessment Tool: Step Four

Finally, but in no way at a linear end, we approached the validity of our study. The one looming threat to our inquiries that we could predict was namely: What if these Extreme Human Overload jokers just didn't care about returning to their group? We chose as a group of educators, students, physicians, scientists, middle school lunch ladies, preacher's ex-wives, pornographic cartoon artists, and generally curious motherfuckers to ignore this one hole in our theory and forge ahead. So, disregarding the question of how valid our projected findings may be, we jumped in.

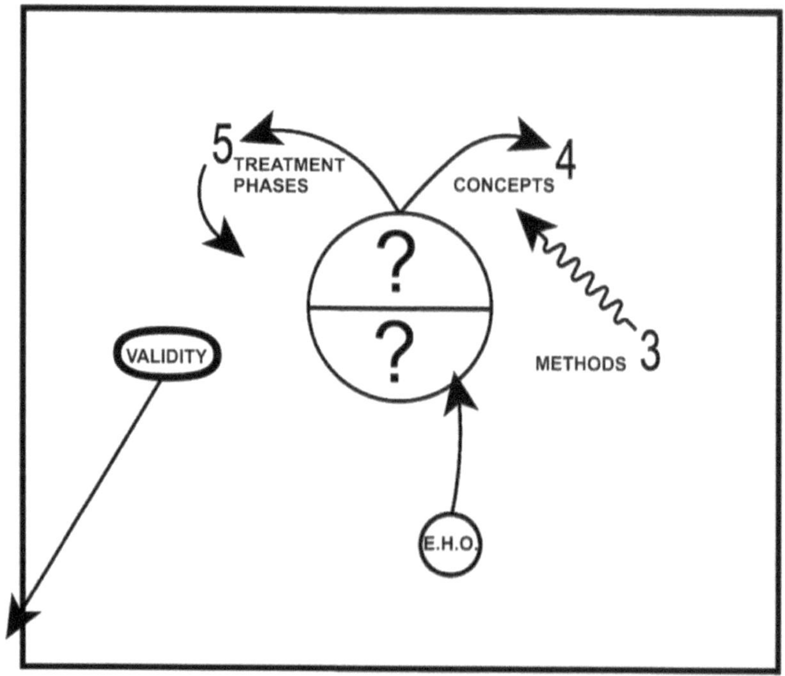

Instititue Assessment Tool: Step Five

In conclusion, but in no way in a straight line from any one point, our model began to take on a resemblance to the 1973 Healthy Buffalo Women's Basketball League's signature isolation play (not to be confused with Buffalo Gals.)

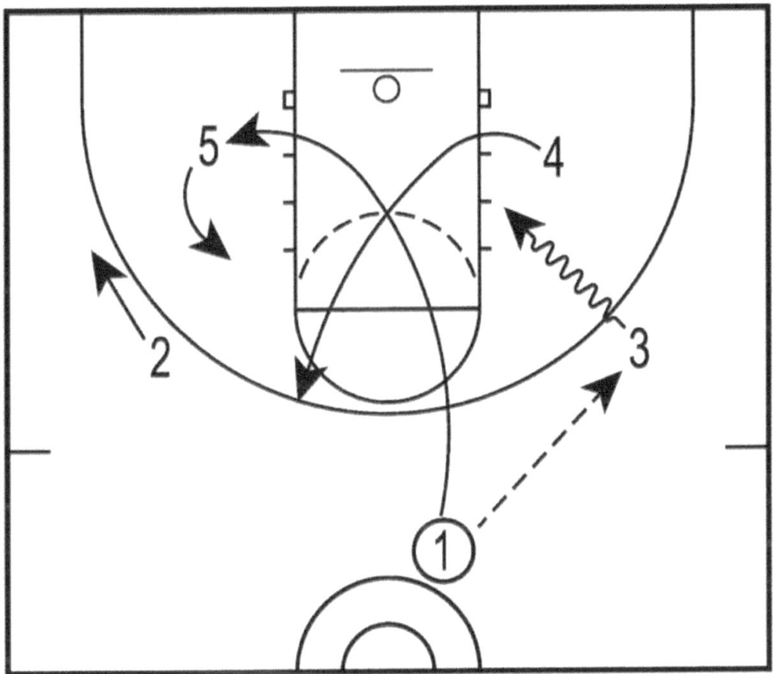

A Jim-Dandy of a Play!

With our model complete, we began almost instantly to see the interrelations of the separate but integrated pieces of our research. Becoming aware of these overlaps lead to a little communication confusion in the initial group sessions with our first test subjects. Our lead examiner, Terrance, made the group aware of the fact that it might be futile to attempt to get those who suffer from the syndrome to reconnect to their groups and they all agreed with him and left. We have tried and cannot track any member of that first group. Terrance has since been put in charge of snacks.

Our paper questionnaires proved challenging. They were administered to large groups in a classroom setting. The lack of personal space and privacy, so deeply important to those plagued by the symptoms of this disease, may have tainted the results just a smidge. Several subjects crumpled their unfinished surveys and hurled them into the group then stomped out. Other questionnaires were also difficult to interpret as a number of them were mistakenly used in the craft room for therapeutic treatment, and many subjects became violent when we attempted to disassemble their origami amusement parks to read the answers to their surveys.

In Appendix A of this volume we've included a sample of the questions processed by our staff and their subjects. The inquiries are designed to present a profile of a person's genesis and how the crowd they came up in changed or changed *them* as they developed*.

---

* We invite you to answer the questionnaire for your own information. Please try to answer truthfully, as if you were taking the exam at our facility. If you complete the exam and are interested in having your answers analyzed, please mail them to:

The Johnston & Johnston Institute

for Guessing What's Wrong With People

42 N. Harms Way, Bumpass, VA 23024.

Please include a stamped, self-addressed envelope for your analysis, as our office supplies were ransacked by Terrance after his demotion.

Electronic computer questionnaires were also incorporated to the screening process as "the internets" and the "world wide web" became more commonplace in the home.

The computer questionnaires were much more telling. We believe that it was the environment in which the subjects were taking these tests that improved our results. It seems that one suffering from Extreme Human Overload would much rather sit in a room by himself to answer questions than just about anywhere else.

Again crossing over toward questioning whether or not our study had any merit in focusing on returning our subjects to their respective groups, these tests unequivocally demonstrated that a great number of our subjects just had no desire to reenlist. We think people, in general, just liked playing on the computer.

The bulk of the data gathered from our research illustrated that these subjects did indeed have some major disconnect from the groups in which they had initially been included.

Not all our test subjects proved to be viable as participants though. Many thought our facility was exploring all manner of group sexual connections, twelve people mistakenly assumed they would get room and board during our trials, and one guy attempted to get us to check off his form for community service. These folks were disqualified from the study leaving only a baker's dozen for our initial trials. But out of the thirteen subjects who actually completed the study, two participants were found to be hiding out from law enforcement, one was just pissed off at his wife for a few hours, one passed away during the =Relaxing Breath Exercise break, and nine were solidly diagnosed with Extreme Human Overload.

Of the nine diagnosed, all agreed to remain enrolled at The Institute for treatment. For the subsequent 6 months following their diagnosis, these subjects were treated with varying recreational therapies, our signature handicrafts, nutritional supplementation (including the controversial "hooch remedy"), individual and group therapy, and letter writing (a form of anonymous venting exercise aimed at releasing animosity felt for the girls in your group, without actually confronting and subsequently alienating them to an even further degree.)

All the above treatment options will be dissected in the chapter on Viable Treatments, but one requires separate and specific handling. As it can be both a cause and a cure, the categorical relationship between alcohol and the Overloader can make for complications when administering the "hooch remedy". With this caveat, we present an exploration in Chapter 5 on E.H.O. and ETOH.

5

E.H.O. & ETOH

ALCOHOL, ETOH, ethanol, hooch, spirits, the sauce, booze, liquid courage, suds, rotgut, firewater, poison, moonshine, tipple, brewski, cold one, bubbly, adult beverage, cocktails, hunch punch, hard stuff, nectar of the gods, or any of the juices, i.e. giggle, happy, or bug, often abused in the name of self medication, this organic compound that binds the hydroxyl functional group to a saturated carbon atom may well contain a metaphorical explanation (as well as a literal one) for its ambiguous place in the treatment and care of those diagnosed with Extreme Human Overload. It is our intolerable binding to our own functional group that can lead us to become saturated sacks of carbon atoms.

As a metabolic byproduct of yeasts and bacteria, alcohol can occur naturally in overripe fruit and grains. And a great many Overloaders are quite familiar with the common grape, hops, barley, and rye varieties. Many patients have admitted that in an effort to "escape" the crowd which has infected them with the Overload, they will begin consuming small amounts of beer or wine at functions that otherwise may prove too uncomfortable. This instinctual maneuver is seen as a hopeful one in the treatment of E.H.O. The subject did not completely abandon the group at the outset. Instead they administered that sweet magic potion that gives us all the liquid courage necessary to face awkward moments. If one is truly plagued with the syndrome, however, they soon find that this small introductory amount is insufficient. In subsequent attempts to manage their desire to split, they may begin consuming alcoholic drinks hours prior to scheduled events. They may continue drinking well after such events have passed. And finally, they may maintain a level of intoxication perpetually to avoid even the *possibility* of having to endure a group exercise. These folks are trying for all they're worth to stick it out! But as their bad luck would have it, this behavior is simply leading them down a road wrought with bonus strife. Many a burgeoning E.H.O. victim has traded the discomfort of the group for alcoholism because it's just easier to explain. Everyone, the world around, knows someone who has been excused from their life second to their addiction to alcohol. Try getting out of your responsibilities by saying you're just tired of being around the people in your life and see where that gets you.

And yet, as fortunate as these intoxicants appear, they have now acquired a second set of problems. The #2 All Time Reason for your people to get all up in your shit is a drinking problem (#1 is having an inappropriate relationship with a pet*.) Developing a dependence on alcohol to manage the anxiety associated with remaining included in your gaggle, will most definitely result in those folks who may have left you alone otherwise, jumping in with both feet to "rescue" you. No sufferer of any syndrome should have to endure invasions on all sides in the name of intervention. But sadly, some victims find themselves trapped between the rock of E.H.O. and the hard place of alcohol addiction.

When faced with this conundrum, one could choose from several options. First, they could quit drinking. In theory, with cases of Class I and some isolated Class II Extreme Human Overload clients, this would initially defuse the added attention from their peers and allow them the temporary space to examine the issues related to their

---

* If you think you may have an inappropriate relationship with your pet, a short quiz has been included in the final section of this book, see Appendix B

E.H.O. We have admitted folks into our treatment facility who first had to be detoxified from and educated on the dangers of alcohol, before they could be properly assessed and treated for their underlying Overload. If upon admission, the patient tests over the legal limit for public intoxication, they are escorted to the 'drunk tank' where we keep them hydrated, comfortable, and safely secured away from the rest of the patients until their blood alcohol returns to pre-soused levels.

The Institute Drunk Tank

Discovered on the building site prior to construction by civil engineers, and proving too much of an expense to remove, The Institute decided to utilize this decomissioned armored vehicle as a temporary detoxification unit to house those patients admitting with blood alcohol levels in excess of the therapeutic range.

The Drunk Tank is a decommissioned army assault vehicle that was uncovered on the clinic grounds during intial site work. You know what they say—"One man's trash is another man's treasure, or in this case, one army's waste is another health facilities great find to help decrease overall costs during a time where we have all been facing massive budget cuts.

These cases are extremely difficult to manage from a clinical standpoint. Families of such sufferers feel it is of the utmost importance to remain involved in the treatment because it appears to be "alcohol related."

This continued presence can derail any attempts at therapeutically encouraging the afflicted individual toward reentering the group. It is imperative in the early phases of treatment for E.H.O. to allow the sufferer a safe measure of distance between themselves and those in their troupe. They must have that time to be left alone to examine their feelings, behaviors, and their consequences. It's the old Catch 22… "How can I miss you, if you don't go away?" Apparently, when people show a compassionate interest in your mental and physical health because of a substance abuse issue, they may feel as if they cannot trust in your complete recovery unless they remain relentlessly involved in it. For this reason we must caution those who would choose this option as the hiatus from this unwanted focus will be short-lived. It has been the experience of our research subjects, treated patients, and our own board of directors that once your family thinks you have a drinking problem they will NEVER leave you alone.

Which brings us to option number two: continue, cut, and run. Now please don't confuse the elements of option two. We don't mean "continue" drinking, "cut" out on the group and "run" for office (so many currently serving congressional figures have misinterpreted this option only to make the most colossal blunders in recent political history…NO DRINKIN' ON THE HILL, mmmkay?!). We mean *continue* on your path to *cut* ties with your assemblage altogether and find some place where no one knows you and you can *run* the rest of your drunken life in peace. Although it may raise an eyebrow in the addiction recovery community, this option is the only way for some Overloaders to keep from creating more damage with their concurrent diseases. By succumbing to the rapture of full blown alcoholism, not only are your Extreme Human Overload symptoms non-issues since you're divorced from your clan, but no one will be there to hound you about your drinking either… win/win!*

This option of course contains no treatment for either malady and should only be utilized in extreme cases of Class III Overload and/or hopeless alcoholics.

---

* It should be noted here that some of our research staff have tried this option for themselves with a modest measure of success, or so we think. Out of the four guys who did it, we've only received correspondence from one —and that was a piece of a bloody postcard from Cabo that can be seen at the end of this volume in Appendix C.

This brings us to the third, and we think the most sensible, choice for those wishing to enjoy a full recovery. This option is to continue to drink in moderation as you explore the therapies designed to treat your Extreme Human Overload.*

As a matter of fact, we here at The Institute believe so much in this option that we encourage moderate drinking even if you've come to treatment without the alcohol on board. We affectionately refer to this drinking as the "Hooch Remedy" and Phase 1 of our 5-Phase Treatment Protocol. We will attempt to explain methods and motives in the coming paragraphs… but first a little belt! Ahhhh. That's good stuff.

One would intelligently surmise that the use of alcohol in treating a syndrome like E.H.O. or any other psycho-social disorder for that matter could be considered risky at best. Add to it the practice of the treating therapists also maintaining a blood alcohol level equivalent to "drunk," in order to regularly administer therapeutic activities and you've got yourself a good, old-fashioned clusterhump. But no small number of marginally good things has been accomplished by those whose peers thought them to be foolish drunks. And as the eminent Winston Churchill once said, "The greatest lesson in life is to know that even fools are right sometimes.†"

"So let's jump off here and do a bit of medical background, shall we?‡

As most mature adults know, and as the NIH so eloquently states in their <u>October 2004, Alcohol Alert,</u>"Alcohol can produce detectable impairments in memory after only a few drinks and, as the amount of alcohol increases, so does the degree of impairment." Now as statements like these seem to have a negative connotation, we like flipping

---

* We must insert here that the professionals at TJ&JIFGWWWP attempted using another substance before landing on the hooch remedy. Admiring all the work Timothy Leary put into studying psychedelics, we planted hallucinogenic mushrooms alongside the vegetables used in food prep for The Institute but were sadly disappointed when on make-you-own-salad-night staff and inmates alike were found wandering naked near the highway, tripping balls.

† Not such a shining salute to our efforts but it never hurts to quote old, dead Brits.

‡ Juuust after one more sip…mmmm!

them to view our glass, no pun intended, as half full. Yes, difficulty walking, blurred vision, slurred speech, slowed reaction times, impaired memory, total indiscretion when hooking up for sex, poor decision making when calling or texting off work for the following day, slapdash vomiting, and a plethora of other missteps are possible and even probable when one partakes in the drink heavily. If the drinker imbibes this much frequently enough though, these issues can become less severe. If the subject is a novice, or worse, an "annual" drinker (enjoying adult beverages only at the occasional celebration, i.e. weddings, New Year's Eve, funerals, casual Fridays, no-pants Wednesdays, etc.) they may be at risk for binging with blackouts. This occurs when you've had more than an over-the-road trucker could tolerate in a weekend, in a matter of a few hours with little time to adjust to the effects. If this occurs outside of a controlled and safe environment, one could surely be at risk for injury. And finally, if drinking is left unchecked in any form, one runs the risk of developing "permanent and debilitating conditions that require lifetime custodial care." – NIH. No way to spin that last statement... it's just a downer.

So armed with the tools listed above, we here at The Johnston & Johnston Institute for Guessing What's Wrong With People set out to use them to the advantage of everyone involved in seeking recovery *from* and offering treatment *for* Extreme Human Overload. In the initial design phases of our treatment facility, the group of benefactors responsible for our creation met for drinks with a local architectural designer and hashed out what amenities the physical building would need. The process of accommodating everyone involved in a treatment facility can be exhausting. The financial backers wanted a pleasing aesthetic, the clinicians wanted privacy, the researchers wanted access to state-of-the-art technological support, the housekeeping staff wanted higher wages, the cooking staff wanted more organics, wild game, and fewer restrictions on cigarette smoking in the kitchen, and the clients wanted to be left out of the whole damn thing altogether! That's an "Overloader" for you! You can imagine it took several meetings and several more cocktails to come to any sort of agreement between all parties. It was in these initial design committee meetings, that the benefits of alcohol were first identified. The money guys were much more liberal with their funds, the designer felt freer to create something wild and beautiful, and the kitchen staff could smoke and drink while contributing to the foundation of our clinic!

We as clinicians began to see the direct correlation between the number of shots these people were consuming and the level of cooperation they were exhibiting. Eureka! If we could incorporate the carefully measured use of alcohol in the treatment of Extreme Human Overload we could not *only* treat these poor dopes, but we could have fun doing it! It is scientifically proven that if you *enjoy* helping people in extreme situations, then you are more effective at it.*

So, as the building was being erected, we began creating our own DSM, including "hooch remedy" as a staple in our treatment playbook.

Our first principal element would have to be that all our boots-on-the-ground staff members would be encouraged to drink daily in an effort to increase their own tolerance so they could maintain a slightly higher blood alcohol level than that of their patients. We established early on in our research that it truly doesn't hurt to be a little scronched when you're trying to help these poor knobs on the daily. And some days being better than others, on the bad days, it's a necessity. Second, when treatment team meetings occur where the therapists and support staff meet to discuss the challenges and progress of each client, it is imperative that we drink. Those meetings have been known to anesthetize even the perkiest of our staff members. Why, Justin used to fall asleep with his mouth full of cheese-n-wheat crackers during treatment team meetings. So, to keep it interesting

---

* As my fortune cookie paraphrased; "If you want happiness for an hour, have a beer; if you want happiness for a lifetime, buy someone else a beer."

and fun, we actually play drinking games while reviewing each individual case.

To demonstrate, we'll put one in place while we continue this text. Every third time we type the word "the," we'll drink!

Cheers!

Since we've often forgotten to record the results of these brainstorming sessions or were unable to decipher our notes afterwards, we have employed the practice of videotaping our treatment teaming to wring every drop of intelligible direction from it. In accordance with our HIPAA regulations, we must wait until every client discussed in our meetings has been discharged before we can post these videos. And since the (drink!) average stay in our clinic is around 3 to 6 months; we try to post new stuff quarterly. Check us out on the YouTube and don't forget to like us and subscribe!

Now our use of alcohol in the direct care and treatment of our clients is much different. When a new client is admitted we initially perform a blood alcohol level examination to determine how much, if any, they have been drinking prior to admission. If it is below the legal limit permitted by the (drink!) Virginia State Police Department, 0.08%, we will immediately administer a therapeutic cocktail. Here we try to accommodate every taste as our patients can be so diverse. We attempt for budgeting purposes to limit our offerings to beer, wine, and whiskey. However, if an individual has already been ingesting one kind of liquor, we will not mix drinks on that individual. No one wants that pukin'-floppy-ass-crying-sister-in-law-type client, especially on the first day. If they admit with a BAC above legal, we ask them when they last drank, where they last drank, if it was very far from here, and if there were many cute prospects there when they left.* The admissions process is time consuming and arduous and we find it's better for everyone if we take the edge off.

As the patient progresses in treatment depending on what therapies he responds best to, we will adjust the (drink!) amount and strength of the hooch. For instance, when first attempting the handicraft portion of treatment, many men become frustrated with following detailed instructions and need a cocktail to ease into the (drink!) activity. And many female clients find the letter writing to be highly emotional and even unbearable if not relaxed prior to the activity with the help of a little nip. Too much alcohol during letter writing, however, can contribute to uncontrollable crying jags or fits of laughter. And, while therapeutic ONCE, these are nothing if not embarrassing and completely irritating to the rest of the group if they occur repeatedly. So again, we measure, we balance, and we administer the (drink!) most therapeutic dose for that client and their specific treatment plan. (Ok... wait. I call timeout on the drinking game for a minute. I'm spinny. That word looks funny, spinny. Issat right? Ok, Bill is going to take over now. He's our designated writer, a.k.a. puss. Take it away, Billy!)

(Ok...what a bunch of assholes!) Well, when we have a client who is anxious about being in treatment, we administer enough to initiate difficulty in walking. If we have begun his nutritional supplementation and we don't want him to read all the ingredients in his Rx Kombeaupaque (Trademarked), we give him enough alcohol to blur his vision. When practicing our

---

* Any Ryan Gosling, Ryan Reynolds, or Meg Ryan-looking fuckers will do.

verbal exercises in group, we will aim for the side effect of slurred speech. (There's really no therapeutic value in this one, it's just more fun for the rest of the group if the speaker is a little boogared up!) Impaired memory is our go to when they've had visitors that turned them off. Just about the only drunken experiences we don't try to recreate are the indiscriminate sex and the vomiting. No indeed, or as Sweet Brown says— "ain't nobody got time for that!"

As we will discuss fully in later chapters, our treatments at the Institute are mostly organic in nature. We attempt to reset the patients' hearts and minds to return to the bosom of their brotherhood without genetically modified means. The nutritional supplementation of which the hooch remedy is a part is made up of naturally occurring vitamins and minerals obtained through the careful preparation of organically raised fruits and vegetables grown right here on our rural campus. All of these efforts are an attempt to detoxify the metabolism of the individual and thus create a healthier physical body to aid in the recovery of the spirit darkened by E.H.O. Our critics bring up the contradiction in our approach, since while a cleansing diet can rid the body's tissues of toxins and create a clearer path to intellectual enlightenment by reawakening the pineal gland, our use of alcohol in treatment will surely "re-toxify" an individual creating more hurdles to overcome.

Now, a brief intermission while we examine the road block the pineal gland presents in the treatment of Extreme Human Overload. The pineal gland is a mysterious endocrine body found deep within the very center regions of the brain. Its release of melatonin, a hormone that influences our sleep/wake cycle and is related to the production of DMT, the "elixir of the pineal gland," possessing the ability to connect our *consciousness in otherworldly ways to planes of other exis-tence, makes this tiny pine cone-shaped structure a fascina-tion. Shamans and yogis around the world have taught their followers how to connect with and use this gland and its hormonal activity to obtain vision beyond our senses in this physical realm. This exceptional perception has been believed to be used to read and even control the thoughts of others. It is precisely this portion of the practice of purifying one's body completely that we cannot support in an effort to help our clients. If someone suffering from E.H.O. could read the thoughts of the people in the gang he was already growing weary of, he might never volunteer for re-inclusion in that gang. And so we clarify the body with good nutrition but cloud the mind with drink. Our clients get better and go home to their families—they really do.*

Ok, Bill. Thanks so much. With that whole mess cleared up, can I just say that while completing this chapter (chapter?…chap

…ter…chapter?…CHAPTER!) we have all been drinking. Except Bill! Ole Billy Boy has remained un-in-e-bri-at-ed! All along! And you cloodn't even tell. I mean you clood NOT tell a shingle ting. We have had soooo many drinksh that we are soooo happy right now. And… uh…wait! Oh…and…um…wait, no wait…we just want you to know that we love you guys. Yesssssssssss we do. We love you. It's not like *love*, love. You know, like sex love. NO! But we love you. And love is the answer. That's what English Dan and John Ford Coppolla said on their alblum Dowton Abbey Road. Lookitup!

Um...Bill here again. They are all asleep now. So we will end today's text with an apology and an introduction to our next chapter on the effects of communication technology on Extreme Human Overload. Trust me; they couldn't even say "communication technology" right now. It's best if they sober up and try again later. Again, I'm sorry and thank you.—Bill

6

Communication Technology and E.H.O.

ONE CANNOT HAVE a conversation about social issues these days without touching on how they relate to communications technology. For example; cyberbullying, personal data breaches, online predators, and my great Aunt Maxine pissing her retirement account away by shopping on her phone after she took too much Ambien. A discussion of Extreme Human Overload is no exception to this rule. Some researchers believe that the advent of the technological age is responsible for great strides in reducing the world's divisions. This is apparent when we remind ourselves that government, industry and academia have all embraced the ideas and developed the concepts of digital telecommunications, personal computers and ultimately the internet. We could probably count on one hand the number of times these entities displayed this kind of joint interest and investment in anything in our own country. Maybe the space program, although the public at large only enjoyed a spectator's role in that in its infancy, certainly not learning about and using the same technology as NASA (except for Tang) until much later. Then there are the many military operations we've gone in on together. But again, the government, or the people who sponsored our government, picked the fights and we sent our young people off to engage, still a really lop-sided relationship. The technologies employed in war are guarded with top-secret clearance, which only serves to widen the gap between the average soldier and his command. Nope, communication technology and its languages and codes are so widely used and accepted that whole factions of our society are actually logged on to the same information together... never have we had such an all inclusive medium.

When the telegraph was invented and began to become widely utilized, our most important messages like birth announcements, deaths in the family, and any other manner of arrival and departure were expedited in a way that had never been imagined before. Our great-great-grandads must have thought this new convenience a modern marvel. Then with the advent of radio, mass messages and information could be transmitted. This would serve to bring small clumps of people together as they gathered around the radio for the transmission of news and entertainment. Then came the telephone. And again we were communicating our most coveted information over great distances in no time at all. As advances in the telephone enabled us to leave a message for someone who wasn't at home or talk on two lines at once, these communications became even more personalized and practical. And then came the mobile phone! Suddenly you didn't even have to be home to share the most important information of the day with your peers, co-workers, or family. Now you could take your telecommunication device with you whenever you were in your vehicle. Indeed with the debut of wireless networks and cellular phones, people are contactable every hour of the day, every day of the year, every minute of their lives, provided they have service where they are. The improvements to the phones themselves have impressed even the most futuristic imaginations in the field. The ability to photograph or video any event or random act has influenced world law and order. As a matter of fact we see this evidenced by the many revolutionary activities around the world that were shared across the internets so that all the human community could bear witness. Of course not every transmission of a photograph or video is worthy of uploading for the world to see. The selfie movement, for example and I think we can all agree, is an exercise in displaying our latent insecurities and the internet might run more effectively if this trend would diminish. Then there are the billions of private parts displayed from phone to phone. I have it on good authority that many folks collect and save whole penis, vagina and breast albums to their devices. I know this may appear prudish advice at best but your phone may not be the best place to store this pornography. Young children who are both fascinated by and quite proficient in their operation, tend to gravitate toward Uncle Toby's phone on the rare occasion that it's left unattended. No one would want the innocence of a small child to be compromised by barraging their senses with a wallpaper array of genitalia, now would we, Uncle Toby? Yes, so you see, along with bringing all sorts of folks together in innumerable ways, we do have some surplus activities of which we could all do with less from our telecommunication devices. It is along the lines of these superfluous goings-on that the flipside of this topic illustrates a complication for those afflicted with E.H.O.

One who is in the grips of the syndrome and is trying desperately to remain included in the mass of society may find it quite stifling to be in constant contact with everyone in the whole wide world at any given time. Before the dawn of the wireless connection, an individual suffering from a bout of Class I could simply take a walk or a drive and distance themselves from the crowd for a while. These types of spontaneous separations are therapeutic and encouraged in the treatment of Extreme Human Overload. However, we have become so physically and emotionally attached to our devices that seldom does anyone ever truly disassociate and leave the actual phone behind. The acronym FOMO (foe-moe) has been allocated for this condition. It stands for Fear Of Missing Out. The intense confusion felt by an individual diagnosed with any of the three classes of E.H.O. who has also been infected with the FOMO, can be debilitating. These folks, though emotionally done with their horde may remain helplessly connected to them. They may compulsively check their phones, emails, Twitter accounts and Facebook pages (no one really does Myspace anymore right?) to make sure they don't miss any smattering of gossip or pictures of someone's gluten-free, vegan, antioxidant tarragon risotto with PINE NUTS! This can be an uphill battle for the patient and the therapists dealing with them.

We take a dual approach to the FOMO client. Obviously, first we take away his phone.

Disconnecting a MO'FO with FOMO in the throes of E.H.O. can sometimes prove to be a no-go.

Now as harsh as this may seem in many advanced cases, we find it imperative to begin with a complete detachment from the devices themselves. Then once the initial reaction (which can be anywhere from total relief to total delirium) wears off we try to reeducate the patient's brain to enter an alternative mindset. We introduce a new acronym for them to try to identify with, namely the DGAF (dee-gaff). DGAF stands for Don't Give A Fuck. And in extreme cases DGAFF or Don't Give A Flying Fuck. With this newly acquired apathy, one can presumably leave his phone or tablet behind and never give it a second thought. This exercise in separation can give our Overloaders small doses of exclusion when necessary without leading them down the road to full on escape, thus keeping them connected with their band if only out of reach for a moment.

There are those who subscribe to the school of thought that the technology of communication today serves to create boundaries between individuals. They say that we are looking into our phones even when we are face to face with a live person with whom we could be interacting. These folks make a good argument for the general public. The attention paid to one's devices rather than the company of those who might contribute valuable interfacing, is lost. Furthermore, the feelings of the ignored individual can be permanently dented. This can lead to harsh judgment of the individual suffering with the FOMO and a disintegration of the relationship altogether.

Very different feelings arise however when one is already suffering a repulsion of those in his company. One infected with Extreme Human Overload sees this type of constant connection through devices with two points of view. First, they feel imposed upon when they can't escape the "ping" of a message every hour, or the vibrating buzz of a call or email while in the middle of a good book. Then there are the notifications on their phones that their Facebook friends need them to look at ANOTHER video of their cats, dogs, kids, extreme weather, yoga pants or other drip of life's trivial puss! These encroachments can prove the proverbial "last straw" in many patients acting on their impulses to express their E.H.O. Countless are the stories in group sessions about the final correspondence a patient received that precipitated their destroying their device and taking it on the lam.*

---

* For example, one group participant, Vernon P. shared that his brother attempted to text him a Happy Birthday message one letter at-a-time over a thirty-two minute span. Needless to say, no one with E.H.O. can tolerate such silly shit and Vernon responded to his brother between the *r* and the *t*, to 'GO POUND SAND!' and then promptly laid his phone down in the driveway and ran over it several times with his babyshit brown 1973 Mercury Montego.

So being on the receiving end of this digital attention can add to these folks bottoming out.

Secondly, when an Overloader is the one who is being ignored by someone presumably present and expecting their individual contribution in a personal interaction, our patient is all too ready to write off yet another one of the "girls in their group" for being *that* person who can't disconnect from their virtual life long enough to live their actual one. As a matter of fact, many of the Institute's patients have described a sort of euphoria that washes over them when they are, "expecting an uncomfortable but necessary personal interaction and it winds up being with one of these rude, inconsiderate, socially inept assholes that couldn't look you in the eye to save their skin." Indeed, our subjects feel relief when another one of the people to whom they are supposed to feel such a connection ignores them at dinner to snap selfies with their blue plate special. They feel an immediate sense of justification in dropping that FOMO Mo'Fo from their ranks. Certainly the Overloader is off the hook – I mean the other guy appears totally disinterested! How can we blame these poor bastards for cutting out when no one even looks at each other over their tuna fish salad sandwich at lunch any more!

Now there are the clients who have never boarded the techno band wagon, so to speak. Your old guys who still have flip phones or dial-up or even the folks who still send actual paper cards and letters (a lost art in my humble opinion). These fellows have a much more difficult time staying connected as they truly can slip off the radar more quickly and with less hullabaloo. Everyone has used the excuse that they were outside their service range or that their phone was acting dumb and dropping calls to avoid calling someone back that they would rather not have to talk to. Honestly, even the most advanced devices behave this way from time to time so this defense can also be a truthful one. But the people still carrying around these phones that look like walkie-talkies— they've got a whole bag of tricks to pull from when they don't want to talk. To follow is a list of actual justifications that patients at our facility have employed to defend their lack of communication in the early stages of Extreme Human Overload.

Excuses – Table 3

- My battery died.
- I was roaming.
- I was going through a ___________. (tunnel, valley, sheep's intestine, etc.)
- I didn't recognize your number.
- I didn't recognize your voice.
- I don't know how to check my messages.
- My phone crashed and all my contacts were lost.
- I was outside and I can't see my screen outside.
- I forgot.
- Your number looks just like my ex-wife's and I never return her calls!
- I forgot to pay my bill and they disconnected my service.
- I was pooping when you called and forgot to call back when I was finished.
- I was asleep when you called and I thought I just dreamed it.
- I was drunk when you called and you are such a buzz kill, I thought I'd wait till I straightened up to call back…and I'm still drunk, so…
- I don't call anyone back who doesn't leave a voicemail message.
- I don't listen to messages left on my voicemail.
- I hate talking on the phone.
- I hate you.
- I hate everyone.

So you can see that even the moderate-low to low tech individuals suffering from E.H.O. can really struggle with the idea of remaining connected when all the fibers in their being are telling them to unfriend every last one of you and head for the hills! These problems are definitely the product of our advancing society so we attempt to establish a way to frame them with gratitude as well as a critical eye. We try to educate our clients on the positive possibilities that come with remaining connected while balancing that with the establishment of healthy boundaries to protect them from the menacing extra overload that comes along with that connection. These boundaries are of course not only beneficial to victims of Extreme Human Overload, but they are also therapeutic for the rest of society. Knowing when to allow the world to creep into our personal space and recognizing when to stop it is a valuable life skill. A little privacy is not always a bad thing. Some things are not meant to be shared by all.*

When we address the technological connection/disconnection within the E.H.O. community, we also acknowledge what a challenge it can be to reach victims and their families. Many people hear about new psychological discoveries and the research and treatment of the disorders associated with them through the public media. Medical documentaries, talk shows, podcasts, and the coverage of news related to any manner of new diagnosis will usually reach droves of folks tuned into TV or radio. And with all these available on the internet now, even the most reclusive may happen across a story that makes him start to put the puzzle pieces together toward identifying his symptoms as part of Extreme Human Overload. However, even if we reach a potential patient or someone in his group, this is only the first layer of a multi-tiered outreach strategy to actually get them to come in for assessment and treatment. We rarely get the client who says, "Yeah I was looking up ways to paint a brick house with a camouflage pattern to make it appear to be an empty lot, when I saw your interview with Dr Kevorkian on www.liveandletdie.com/disappearing-podcast." It's never that simple. Usually, these people or someone they know sees the initial broadcast of an informative interview with scientists or physicians or colorful yet annoying local daytime talk show hosts and their interest is piqued. Maybe we described a symptom they had or a scenario to which they related and the seed was planted. Then we discovered, after breaking out with our findings

---

* You're no less authentic for keeping your shirt on during Mardi Gras than you are if you show'em your tits (unless you feel compelled to do so by your authentic self). But just because you do feel compelled to do something doesn't mean that the rest of us want to see the pictures.

in a media blitz (in the Piedmont Uplands) to which not a single soul responded, we needed to launch follow up strategies after every such exposure. Many of the Overloaders themselves do not respond to traditional means of advertising. Our public relations people have had nightmare after nightmare when it comes to failed publicity campaigns. We went big first with billboards found along the Blue Ridge Parkway, thousands of people driving by… and nothin'. It seems our victims are in such poor psychological shape that many of them drive with the posture of a plastic bag filled with vegetable beef soup and rarely look anywhere but straight ahead when they drive and almost never lift their heads when they ride! Then with the knowledge of this eyes-straight-ahead piece, we tried bumper stickers. But as everyone knows, you cannot print a large amount of information on a 3"x12" strip of vinyl adhesive. So our initial efforts were products like, "Hate Everyone? We can help." J&JIFGWWWP 1-866-FOR-HATE. These were completely ineffective and spiked a number of militia-based hostage situations for which we narrowly escaped blame. So we tried, "Tired of the girls in your group? Let us help you with your connections" J&JIFGWWWP 1-866-FOR-LOVE. This, as you can imagine, led to a full blown investigation of our facility by the Bumpass Municipal Vice Squad/Prostitution Division as well as the Virginia Commonwealth Authority of Bumper Sticker Safety and Crime Prevention. But this did not deter our P.R. team.* Eventually we were able to post informative snip-its on beer cans and cigarette cartons.†

Our low-tech approaches turned out to be the only ones our clients responded to. They didn't like us on Facebook, they didn't follow us on Twitter, and we couldn't *buy* a hashtag‡ to save our lives!

---

* It only encouraged them. A group of our staff rose to the challenge and went to the mattresses to lobby a compromise between the tobacco and alcohol suppliers to run our ads in exchange for a reduction in the tobacco and alcohol taxes sought after by local legislators. It turns out many of our state's delegates were among those suffering from E.H.O. and they compassionately lent their support.

† We did have to agree to use each vendor's product who ran our ads in the facility itself, but the cooks do smoke a lot and we needed the hooch anyway.

‡ Hashtage are something you can buy, right?

But that's ok.* Even with all the advances at our disposal, sometimes the best way to reach someone is by word of mouth – and that shit's free! So many of our clients were simply brought around to the clinic by someone who had benefited from our treatment and recognized that need in someone else.

We could conclude that our connection with connecting is inevitable and useful and maddening and great and awful. At The Institute our efforts continue to reach and care for our client base without putting them off and simultaneously utilize the latest advancements in the digital environment.

---

* As it turns out, you can't actually buy a hashtag. At least that is what our tech team has been telling us. So we don't have any choice except for it to be ok.

7

Viable Treatments

WHILE SOME OF the folks suffering from Extreme Human Overload are helped and others hindered by the advancements in the digital world, most of the modalities we employ at The Institute to treat them are an honest throw-back to the colloquial *old school*. We utilize the simplest methods of hands-on therapy available since the ancient Egyptians cut the papyrus with the first primitive scissors. In this chapter we will outline each element of our 5 Phase Treatment Protocol including the rationale behind each phase. All classes of E.H.O. engage in each phase, in order. And no, this is not a cookie cutter approach to our clients as each individual spends his own customized time allotment within each phase. If one is suffering from Class I disease, they may remain in Phases 1-4 for only hours or days but require weeks or months in Phase 5 to successfully complete treatment. Conversely, if we are lucky enough to enroll a Class III victim, they may need prolonged exposure to Phase 1 just to keep them in treatment long enough to *get* to the other phases. But by keeping the therapy order consistent, we can more easily track and adjust our format for ongoing research and continuous improvement in the field of guessing what's wrong with people. Since Phase 1: Hooch Remedy has already been discussed at length in Chapter 5 (and we're really very sorry for the embarrassing manner in which it was) we will begin with Phase 2: Paper Roses.

Phase 2: Paper Roses – Inherent in the psyche of everyone with E.H.O., no matter the classification of symptoms, is the desire to be left alone. The degrees of this mindset are as varied as the individuals themselves. Some folks need weeks alone to decompress before they can be persuaded to join any group activity while others respond well after only hours away from their core group and are ready for remedial entry in small cells of new acquaintances. But as we are in the business of creating the desire in all our clients to re-enter completely, we must construct a diversion of sorts to the very solitude they crave.

Our Phase 2 desensitization-reeducation pods are 10'x10' square isolation rooms customized to our clients' comfort level. They may choose from a pallet of calming colors for the walls, a collection of natural textiles for the floor covering, and a group of lounge furnishings with accessories ranging from comfy pillows to luxurious throws. These hammocks, chaises, recliners, sofas, and even beds are equipped with a detachable "writing desk" style craft tray, with a keyed security mechanism that can only be removed by designated staff members. Each pod is virtually soundproof and equipped with a skylight and fresh air vents to circulate warm or cool air throughout the pod. Individualized aromatherapy scents are wafted into the ventilation ducts to maximize the tranquil effects of the environment. The participant can request the room be darkened or more illuminated depending on their preference for relaxation. And finally a whisper soft playing of Anita Bryant and the Monty Kelly orchestra's 1960 popular music hit, *Paper Roses* is piped into speakers. This white noise is looped repeatedly but so softly played that it barely registers with the client's conscious mind. As a matter of fact, few if any clients even mention the music in the feedback evaluation portion of this step.

For a minimum of the first five days in treatment, each individual is required to spend one hour in the morning and one hour in the evening in the pod. During this introductory period, their customized environment is recreated exactly as they designed it upon admission. They may even incorporate their Phase 1 cocktails into their Paper Roses Pod time for this initial period, but they are forbidden from eating or drinking anything else during these intervals. After each session, the clients are asked for feedback about their "quiet time." After each day, sessions are increased or decreased depending on the range of comments indicating whether or not an individual is prepared for the next step of treatment. Times are limited to no less than one hour and no more than four. Once forward progress is recognized, the time in the pod is set at that same interval throughout the rest of Phase 2.

The Overloader is then instructed by recreational therapists in a private therapy/class room to view five different YouTube videos on how to make paper flowers. They then choose their favorite, and the therapist equips them with the supplies to create as many flowers as they think they can in their set pod interval. The therapist works with the Overloader to master the craft before the next step. With a positive return demonstration, the client is returned to the pod with their craft supplies and instructed to begin creating flowers.

Upon beginning this step in Phase 2, Phase 1 cocktails are no longer permitted. This simple implementation begins the desensitization of the individual. Feedback is measured following this step of treatment. It should be noted that Phase 1 cocktails continue throughout other portions of therapy, but are strictly curtailed during this exercise. By just removing the alcohol from this exercise, many Class I and II sufferers beg to be graduated from the solitude of the pod. But there are still those too sick to care who require more drastic measures to break their loner boner. For these hard cases, the therapy advances.

If a person is not phased by the load of craft work before them and is undaunted by facing that load without liquid refreshment, day by day we begin to reverse their environment. First, we place them in a pod of a different color than they initially chose. The next day, we put them in one with a different rug on the floor. And each subsequent day we change their familiar space from one of their own making to that of one which was chosen for them. This can serve to create a quiet discomfort they then associate with being alone. If this still does nothing to deter them, then their choices for heat or cold and light or dark are reversed. Now they are operating in a 10'x10' room of someone else's taste in unfavorable lighting and temperature. If this still does nothing to encourage them to leave their solitude, we add essential patchouli oil to the aroma therapy.* But in the unlikely event that even *that* does not produce therapeutic results there is one final step in this phase that has proven unbeatable.

It should be noted here that in all the years since we got our licensure back,† 97.13% of our clients have successfully completed Phase 2 without this final step. But there have been a couple of asshats that just had to push the envelope. Their feedback can be found in Appendix D of this book, entitled <u>The Letters</u>. Once the final step has been initiated, all staff and clients are led to other wings of the building as the screaming is the only thing we've found that can be heard outside the soundproofing of the pods. In the final steps of Phase 2, we increase the volume of the background music to an easily audible level, continuously looping Anita Bryant's *Paper Roses*. This is done for both daily sessions for two days. Upon the third day, if no indication of relenting is evident, we replace the Anita Bryant version with the 1973, Marie Osmond, country-pop version of the same song! Now, I know what you're thinking… and yes we've had people all over us from Amnesty International to Human Rights Watch to John McCain, and they've all agreed that although this measure does sound torturous to the rest of us, some of these hard cases would be lost if

---

* Come on, even the potheads have to hate the smell of that!

† Just shy of our fifth anniversary of accreditation by the World Treatment Foundation or W.T.F., Terrance (staff) and Wedding Dress Jerome (long-term patient) were found alone in the drunk tank contracting each other's gingivitis. As this was Terrance's third strike, his employment was terminated on the spot but not before an anonymous tip was sent to the W.T.F., closing us down for six months of staff training and facility wide dental hygiene examinations.

we didn't have a "big gun," so to speak. It seems that inclusion in even the worst group is not as miserable a fate as sitting alone in a room, locked into an easy chair and forced to make tissue paper flowers while listening to Marie Osmond sing. This final step in Phase 2 marks the beginning of the long, long road to recovery for those afflicted with Extreme Human Overload and ushers in the next phase.

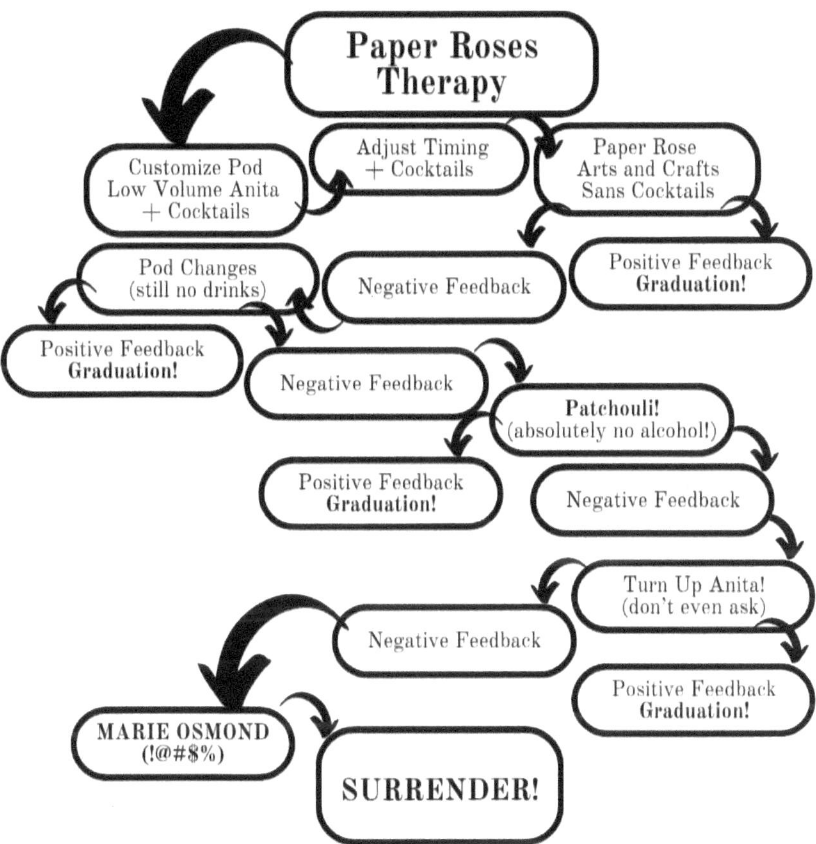

The Johnston & Johnston Institue for Guessing What's Wrong With People's Official Flow Chart for Phase II Paper Roses Therapy Treatment.

Phase 3: Sewing Clothes for Pets – Desensitizing one from enjoying solitude only serves to get our clients physically back into a group dynamic. It doesn't, however, return their hearts and minds to a place of caring or empathy. Phase 3 is designed to rebuild their "give a damn" and thus create positive feelings directed toward the assembly. Our treatment teams brainstormed for months to try to come up with a charity or cause that we could get our clients around to increase their humanity, but repeatedly when sample groups of clients were exposed to groups of other people who needed anything from them, they closed down faster than an Iranian restaurant deep in the heart of Dixie! Time and again, when people were the focus of their acts of kindness, our clients found ways to be less than kind. The E.H.O. victim reaches a point in their relationships where they simply have no desire to relate to anyone else on their team. They are tired of looking at things through the eyes of others to try to understand their behavior or help with their problems. Reaching this point is often the catalyst that brings about the onset of symptoms. So once Phases 1 & 2 have been successfully executed Phase 3 is initiated to return a sense of empathy to our clients.

In developing our program we tried many methods for encouraging empathy. We explored the word itself in group sessions opening the floor for everyone's own definition of the term. We've seen that many folks learn new concepts by framing them their own way. But the true victims of E.H.O. have such an aversion to "other" that their *in-their-own-words* definitions turned out to range from troubling to laughable. Table 4 illustrates some of the feedback we repeatedly get in group sessions. We share this with you here to demonstrate the degree to which this disease affects even the brightest and most sincere Overloaders. It should be noted that in their defense, they were given no context from which to work–but still? Each erroneous term is defined following the patient's interpretation for clarification.

Table 4

Brad C. <u>Empathy</u> – the name of the character meaning and. (&) {ampersand}
Jeff C. <u>Empathy</u> – the rear part of an airplane. {empennage}
Gail P. <u>Empathy</u> – a measure of the unavailable energy in a thermodynamic system. {entropy}
Luann N. <u>Empathy</u> – eager desire for relief or change, restlessness. {impatience}
Barbara F. <u>Empathy</u> – lack of reverence for God, ungodliness. {impiety}

Obviously we had our work cut out for us. So, after educating our groups on the actual definition of the word, we explored ways in which to illustrate this definition. We showed countless documentary films featuring displaced families, orphaned children, and lone survivors of natural disasters, all subjects that would move the average person to tears of empathetic concern. This failed to affect even those suffering with the mildest cases of Extreme Human Overload. We then invited guest presenters to relate in person their touching stories of loss and recovery. Many with tales of losing one's entire family or village–still nothing. Then one of our research interns happened to observe a client on the grounds outside her lab window, freeing an acorn from the gravel path to aid a squirrel waiting in a tree nearby. That was IT! If we couldn't get our population to regard their human counterparts empathetically, maybe we could introduce the concept through a relationship with animals.

. . .

We surveyed our subjects with such inquiries as:

1. If your building is on fire and you only have time to rescue one living thing do you go for _______________?
    A) your brother-in-law
    B) a 25 year-old, paralyzed, diabetic, stray dog with cataracts
    C) your spouse

2. When confiding in someone your darkest thoughts and secrets do you choose _________________?
    A) Your mother
    B) Your psychologist
    C) Harry, your iguana

3. You're lost and alone on a highway at night, you run out of gas, do you _____________________?
    A) Walk to the nearest house and ask for help
    B) Call someone from AAA, your sponsor from AA, or your friend Aaron for assistance
    C) Follow a large, dark, cat-like animal off the road and into the underbrush

Consistently these bitches chose the animal time and time again!

So, our work shifted to the introduction of therapy animals. We contracted dogs and cats from aideson4legs.org to encourage a loving, empathetic response between patient and service animal. But our efforts were in vain. Even when our clients appeared interested (which we calculated to be about 27.91% of the time) the animals were not having it. With yet another failed attempt but unwilling to give up on the animal connection, we stepped back for a fresh perspective. How could our E.H.O. patients offer compassionate support to another living thing without coming in direct contact with it? That's when Everett the custodian began to complain about the amount of wasted paper thrown out during our Phase 5 origami therapies and suggested we use the scraps to make patterns for clothes for the therapy animals.

When it comes to design, your imaginiation is the only limit!

As stupid as this sounded at first, we *were* out of ideas, and it *would* incorporate the animals we had already contracted, and we *did* waste an awful lot of paper. So we said, "What the hell!" We employed Everett's wife, Wilma Dean to instruct the clients on properly measuring and fitting our four legged friends* with comfy gym clothes, suits, coats, sweaters, and sleepwear.

With every new animal fashion created, each client's empathy began to slowly grow and develop until they could easily relate to the

---

* One of our Class III clients, second to several untoward interactions with the mammals, was directed on how to make a wedding dress for a live perch we bought from a red-headed middle schooler behind the fish market in downtown Bumpass. "Wedding Dress Jerome" will be celebrating his 13th year in residence at our facility, our longest clinical relationship to date.

animals and Everett and Wilma Dean as well. Once on the road to "feeling" something again, we progress to Phase 4.

Phase 4: Letters – It is common practice in the psychology community for therapists to encourage their patients to compose a letter to someone they may feel animosity, jealousy, anger, or just general bitterness toward in an effort to rid the composer of these debilitating emotions. The treatment for Extreme Human Overload is the perfect instance for this technique. Our clients have overcome their need for solitude, have grown some semblance of empathy and are now ready to tackle some of the issues present in the relationships that pushed them away from the center of their groups. When a client reaches Phase 4 they are encouraged to choose any number of important people to write to. They are prompted to write as much or as little as is necessary to accurately portray their true feelings to each recipient. Then our clients are asked to read and reread these letters over and over again until they have disassociated their negative feelings from the people toward which they were aimed. With this step complete, they are then asked to destroy the letters by placing them in the outdoor pizza oven on 'fire night;' ceremoniously ending their antisocial emotions towards others in their group. The release our clients experience with this exercise is nothing short of miraculous, but the letters illustrate that better than any explanation could, so we've included samples of actual client letters in Appendix D of this volume for your examination. Each one represents hours of soul searching and healing.*

Phase 5: Origami Architecture – Finally we've arrived at the final stage of treatment, Phase 5. This is such a significant integrative tool for our Overloaders. This is the portion of treatment where they literally construct a new group setting of which to become a part. We

---

* Phase 4 is one of my personal favorites!

spend hours training them to fold countless pieces of paper in the ways of the ancient artists to create homes, offices, stores, and neighborhoods! They work to symbolically create a new community for themselves to reenter. As they work in small groups and in individual sessions creating these paper worlds, they process the benefits of being part of the crowd again. They recognize the merits of belonging and begin to plan their actual return to their assemblage. Many make such astounding progress that they actually plan their own welcome home parties complete with guests, decorations, nibbles, drinks, games, and everything! Some go big and include places they'd never gone before like the mall or the races. While others map more modestly, only planning to return to a select number of family and friends. It's important to note once again that no two Overloaders recover in the same manner. But with this practice in environmental reconstruction, even the worst afflicted can be made ready to rejoin his troop. Once the fifth and final phase of treatment is successfully completed, we begin the process of integrative discharge. This takes the coordination and cooperation of the individual client and the folks to whom he will be returning. In the next chapter we will examine one's supporters and the major role they play in helping their loved one recover from E.H.O.

8

Support for Overloaders: A Tricky Proposition

So, you find yourself close to someone who has been diagnosed with Extreme Human Overload and you want to know what to do to help. At the onset of treatment, friends and family are given one set of instructions, the very same set for every patient's group no matter what class of disease with which they present, no matter how severe or mild their symptoms, no matter what. This directive is succinctly referred to with the acronym BTFO, otherwise known as BACK THE FUCK OFF! The people succumbing to the ravages of E.H.O. have found themselves in a terrible place. They have, through no fault of their own, become swollen with bitterness and venom. They find themselves avoiding the people they love the most or blasting them with the boiling bile that they feel rising in their necks every time they are in their midst. The very last thing anyone in this position needs is someone asking if they're "okay" or "what can I do?"

"Are you ok?" is the most detrimental question to ask anyone suffering from E.H.O. Literally any other question would be more useful.

BTFO people, it's not about you! First of all, no one needs to be "okay" all the time anyway. You don't have to have a diagnosis of E.H.O. to have a bad day and not feel like entertaining everyone. Second, at the onset of symptoms, there really isn't a whole helluva lot you *can* do. We tell significant others who've brought their partner in for assessment or admission that the behavior exhibited by someone stricken with Extreme Human Overload can be so caustic and vile that the only advice we can give is to take nothing personally. When the victim is truly in the throes of the syndrome they can behave with such a disconnect to their normal selves that they aren't even aware of their actions. One cardinal rule of therapy for our clients is that when they experience such episodes, they need to practice repeating the words, "I love you. I'm sorry. I love you. I'm sorry." This repetition seems to serve as a gentle reminder that they are still human and deserve a chance to get better and return to their place in the pack.

Upon completion of treatment, each client is asked to compose a list of the people previously in their group that they think would want them to return. This is the support network we begin with. When your loved one is ready to begin their integrative discharge, if you've made the list, you will be asked to come in for several sessions.[*]

First you will be interviewed alone by staff. This helps us to know if you are going to be a help or a hindrance to our client's recovery. Then you will meet with staff and the client jointly. Then finally you will be asked to attend group sessions with other significant others.

In the initial session with staff you need to honestly grade your connection to know your place in this person's circle. If you recall the analogy made in Chapter 1 about the target,[†] you will understand that if the Overloader is in the bullseye and you are, say, at the two point ring, there is a great chance that your relationship will not survive even after treatment is successfully implemented. However, if you are indeed included in the center ring with him or in an adjacent ring, you should most definitely expect to resume contact upon completion of treatment. And this variance in the part you take in someone's life is directly correlated to the actions you can take to support the victim. We created the Significant Other(s) Scale to help folks identify themselves and determine what their level of support should be. These relationships are graded from 1 being the least significant, to 10 being the most. Table 5 demonstrates the caliber of connections and how they can be affected by E.H.O. Each grade is followed by a brief description of the kind of relationship it may represent.[‡]

---

[*] Incidentally, if you did not make the list, you will receive a form letter from our clinic stating that you will no longer be counted among the flock of the Overloader and you need to seek out others to befriend.

[†] Go back to page 2 for a refresher. Remember page 2? That was so long ago. We were so young, weren't we?

[‡] You may note that there is no place on the scale for adult children. This is due to the

Table 5

#1 – <u>Friend of an Acquaintance</u> – You met while accompanying an acquaintance of the victim past his campsite. This is beyond the outer margin of the circle and you are not a significant other.
#2 – <u>Acquaintance</u> – You only met the victim once or twice and we really don't think she could pick you out of a line up, so… piss off!
#3 –<u>Friend of a Friend</u> – You are friends with a friend of the victim. You have never spent time alone or initiated contact with the victim directly. Again this relationship is only marginal, don't expect a call.
#4 – <u>Friend</u> – You have worked with the victim or have been to his home on your own. You each saved the other's number in your phone and are friends on social media with restrictions. You can expect to resume some level of contact again after treatment, but don't be pushy. Take what you can get.
#5 – <u>Cousin</u> – We use "cousin" here to represent any familial relationship outside parents and siblings. You are someone the victim will be thrown with at weddings and funerals and if you were reasonably close before you can expect your relationship to return to normal.
#6 – <u>Parent</u> – We would like to think that all parents and their children would be reunited after treatment, but if you are a parent you know that you often get blamed (fairly or un) for the ills of all so it's a crapshoot for you.
#7 – <u>Sibling</u> – If you've been there for your brother or sister through it all, expect to resume your normal relationship. If you've been an asshole too, consider treatment for yourself or don't even bother calling.
#8 – <u>Lover</u>* – If your relationship was purely sexual, you probably didn't stick around after your partner started showing signs of E.H.O., so never mind.
#9 – <u>Spouse</u>* – Once the preexisting condition of a failing marriage is ruled out, you can count on the victim returning to you with love in their hearts for you. If you were on the rocks anyway–see ya!
#10 – <u>BFF</u>* – You are the only person the client really needs to get back in the good graces of. Thank you for being patient and please try to forgive the victim for everything they put you through. They *do* love you and they *are* sorry.

*These positions can be held by three separate individuals or one or two
persons can occupy any combination of the three.

Now, once you've made the cut, you can begin to process some of the behaviors you and your loved one can practice to support their recovery and prevent any relapse. You will learn from your Overloader things that you do to irritate them, stuff they never want to do again, things they'll never ask of you again, and so on. You will also learn what they have learned about what triggers them to want to run

---

fact that no matter how your kids act or react to you, you always have to be there for them. Oh! They can drop *you* like a hot rock, but you can *never* stop loving them. So suck it up and keep crying in the shower.

away and the skills they have acquired to keep them in place. These things can be as simple as taking solo walks after work or leaving the radio off during short car rides to cut down on sensory overload. Learn them, practice them. Know none of this is your fault or yours to fix. But most importantly, know that your loved one has gone to great lengths to get better and get back to you. So don't cock it up. Be patient. Be forgiving. And when in doubt, BTFO!

9

My Story

As unconventional as it may seem, this final chapter will serve as an introduction of sorts. I am Deidre Johnston, N.D.P.G.,[*] the co-founder of the Johnston & Johnston Institute for Guessing What's Wrong With People and the author of this collective work on Extreme Human Overload. In Chapter 2: Who Is At Risk For E.H.O.? and in the dedication of this volume, I elude to two women without whom this work would have remained in my underpants drawer, far from anyone who could have benefitted from it. The women are my sister, Midge, and myself a.k.a. Ms. D. It is our story of kinship and courage that follows.

Our childhood was atypical of the late 60's early 70's American variety. Our parents were not hippies or activists. They were more 1950's style than was prevalent at the time. Our dad worked hard, sometimes multiple jobs at once and our mom was pretty and fun. We lived in a single family household in a family-friendly neighborhood, and walked or rode bikes everywhere. We were blessed with the essentials and even some of the nonessentials. We had each other, a younger brother and much extended family. We had it all. And we

---

[*] Non-Doctrinated Professional Guesser

were happy people. And I felt loved not just by my family, but by my entire community–bullseye!

As did a lot of folks, I thought of my childhood fondly and sought to provide my own family with one similar. My life progressed, and unfortunately for my first born children (both amazing half-Swedes), I was too young and immature when I had them. I chose husbands poorly, more than once and struggled to give them the kind of upbringing I wanted for them. My quest to create the kind of carefree and nurturing family I always wanted was dashed by disappointment after disappointment. I had awoken from the dream that was my own childhood. Things were good enough, but they weren't, as they never truly are, as fan-freakin-tastic as they seemed. So, through many trials, failures and recoveries my little family and I bungled our way until we *all* reached adulthood. There is really something to be said for waiting to make the big decisions in your life until your brain fully develops.[*] Then as luck or karma or whatever brings us to new lives would have it, I met and married a man who possessed the key to my soul. My husband, number four,[†] turned out to be the finest man I know. He taught me the meaning of respect and brought out the very best in me. We were peers. And he remains the most important support in my life. We met oddly and inconveniently late in our lives, but despite the timing were able to bring a little girl into this world. My daughter proved to be an inspiration beyond anything I had known. She is my joy and my favorite person. My heart breaks with regret every day knowing that she's better because I am more mature and can teach and learn from her more effectively than I did when my little Swedes were young. Regret, my sister says, is a four-letter word worse than "fuck." The ongoing recovery from the guilt of messing up with my kids continues to be my greatest challenge. And may well have been the catalyst for the onset of my own E.H.O.

Because I've learned to "always do what comes next" – George

---

[*] See All State commercial - Chapter 2

[†] The fortune teller told me he would be number four of five, but I reject that on the grounds that I could see the cord to her crystal ball.

Carlin, my family and I accepted our latest new direction and began building toward the staples we thought were required for forward progress. I changed careers moving out of crime scene cleaning and into massage therapy, a common transition. I started a small business and opened an urban salon in the vacant apartment below ours. Although I amassed yet another group to impress, my massage clients, I struggled with the usual ups and downs of trying to launch a service business and after three years was unable to keep it afloat. I closed my doors and took a position in my old massage therapy school as an anatomy instructor; again, growing more respected with every exposure to each new class of students. With a more reliable income to add to my husband's, we were able to save for a modest home in the suburbs, close to my daughter's school, complete with a pool in the backyard! We really felt as if we had it all. Our desires were few and our blessings were many.

We went right to work readying the pool for family and friends and began hosting an interminable cookout that would last all that summer.

Shortly after the season ended, I began to experience changes in my composure. I had always been brutally honest and outspoken, but I thought I was at least kind. And with this emotional shift, brutal was the only thing I remained of the three things I listed in that last sentence. I was vitriolic and venomous with my tongue. I was ill tempered and ridiculously over sensitive. I thought my husband went from smart and clever to direly unfunny and pointedly cruel with his humor.* Throughout the holiday season and to the end of that first year, I avoided as many gatherings as I could without raising suspicion. I was morphing and I didn't know what to do about it.

After a particularly rage-fueled verbal attack on my husband, I sent myself to my room to keep the collateral damage to a minimum and called my big sister, Midge. I laid it all out for her, the mood swings, the insomnia, the fatigue, the anger, the lack of a sensible filter and she listened intently to my laundry list of bad behavior.

Then quietly and definitively she spoke the words, "You have the E.H.O." I stopped my sobbing and asked her to repeat herself. She did and she continued to explain that Extreme Human Overload was what she had dubbed this series of emotional unravelings that she too had experienced off and on for roughly the last two years. We immediately correlated the onset of our symptoms to the two most common causative factors for women with Overload; perimenopause and trouble with adult children.

---

* He had not.

"Oh Midge, what's wrong with me?"
"Sister, you've got the E.H.O.!"

Over the next few weeks and months, we commiserated, relating tales of unrelenting symptoms and anxiety-producing guilt. Indeed, it was Midge who taught me the I'm sorry-I love you mantra. She was ripe with advice and her own stories of disconnection. Midge's case differed only in the fact that she was already hundreds of miles away from close friends and family, having moved out of state years prior to the onset of her disease. As she did not invest in her new community to the degree with which she had in her previous relationships, she was able to remain somewhat aloof in her new home. But she did work as a ticket supervisor at the Bouncy House and Teddy Bear Boutique which put her in daily contact with children and their parents, not to mention a cast of coworkers that were all drawn to her, as was everyone she met. I acquiesced on the burden I'd found myself carrying to be one of the Johnston Sisters all the time. I related that I was tired of doing the Deidre Show. It was exhausting to be the positive, up-beat, wise and entertaining one of every group. I had real pain in my life. I was grieving broken relationships with people very important to me. I didn't feel like being nice anymore!

It is at this juncture that I need to reveal that our maternal grandmother had displayed undeniable signs of being afflicted with this same malady since we were children. But as kids will do, we allowed ourselves to be distracted by Hawaiian Punch and Little Debbie Swiss

Cake Rolls. Later in life, after learning from our mother what horrible behavior she had witnessed in *her* mother, we would jokingly refer to our grandmother as The Black Heart–and *she* wasn't as bad as *her* mother before her. So, we were perplexed. Did this antisocial behavior arise second to the hormone fluctuation of looming menopause? Did we find it discouraging to give and receive love and respect from friends and acquaintances when we lacked it in some of the other, more important relationships in our lives? Did we learn it from watching our beloved grandmother? Did we inherit it? Did we all have a piece of The Black Heart in us? It was this plethora of unanswered queries that prompted me to gather my colleagues and begin what has been a noble quest in the development of the diagnosis and treatment of Extreme Human Overload. And although Midge is the second Johnston in the clinic's nomenclature, she still suffers so intensely from her own symptoms of E.H.O. that she refuses to become a part of it. She just cannot bear to be associated with yet another group of people she is sure she'll grow weary of and attempt to leave behind. Her wisdom far outweighs her annoying exclusion. I have not given up on finding a way to help her. I am toying with a Home Health division to offer the clinical therapies available at The Institute in the homes of individuals as well as a do-it-all-by-yourself-kit that may be beneficial to those holed up in tough-to-reach spots. Just like the NASCAR guys have helped everyday driving technology, we have been able to share our research and treatment techniques with other disciplines within the medical, scientific, and criminal justice communities to help those suffering a myriad of other disorders as well. Heroin addicts respond well to a version of the Paper Roses therapy. First-time dogfighting offenders have been rehabilitated by our Sewing Clothes for Pets panacea. And of course, the Letters continue to prove paramount to the recovery of countless immature assholes that just can't help but carry old grudges to the nth degree.

So, what began as a bitch session between sisters has mushroomed into a renowned organization reaching out to disenfranchised individuals everywhere in an effort to re-enfranchise them. Our research is ongoing and our clinicians remain steadfast in the search for more and better ways to keep our society intact. We, as the human group, must find more effective methods of sticking together if we are to share this planet and her resources fairly. For all our intellect and advancement, we still haven't found a better way than working together toward our common goals. It is the pointed design of my life's work and The Johnston & Johnston Institute for Guessing What's Wrong With People to offer solutions to overcoming the disconnection of Extreme Human Overload and to further the cause of a humanity reunited for the good of all!

Appendix A
RESEARCH QUESTIONNAIRE

Research Questionnaire #1

Subject Number: _______________   **Gender: M/F/T/N**   **Age:** ______

1. Were your parents married when you were born?	YES ☐ go to #3	NO ☐ go to #2
2. Did they marry after you were born?	YES ☐ go to #3	NO ☐ go to #4
3. Did they marry each other?	YES ☐ go to #6	NO ☐ go to #4
4. Did they marry significant others who helped to raise you?	YES ☐ go to #6	NO ☐ go to #5
5. Who raised you anyway? Mom? Dad? Split custody? Other?	YES ☐ <u>good!</u> YES ☐ <u>good!</u> YES ☐ <u>BEST!</u> YES ☐ ok…	NO ☐ <u>sorry…</u> NO ☐ <u>sorry…</u> NO ☐ <u>so sorry.</u> NO ☐ ok…
6. Did this union last your entire childhood?	YES ☐ go to #7	NO ☐ go to #8
7. Was it a happy one?	YES ☐ go to #9	NO ☐ go to #9
8. Did you have anything to do with its demise?	YES ☐ go to #11	NO ☐ go to #12
9. Did you have siblings within this union?	YES ☐ go to #13	NO ☐ count your blessings!
10. Everyone skip this question.	✖	✖
11. Are you proud of yourself, you little shit?	YES ☐	NO ☐

12. Are you sure?	YES ☐ ok then.	NO ☐ go back to #8
13. Were you the oldest?	YES ☐ LUCKY! go to #16	NO ☐ HA! HA! go to #17
14. Were you the youngest?	YES ☐ LUCKY! go to #16	NO ☐ HA! HA! go to #17
15. Were you the middle child?	YES ☐ sorry… go to #17	NO ☐ LUCKY! go to #16
16. Were you a happy child?	YES ☐ go to #18	NO ☐ go to #19
17. Were you an unhappy child?	YES ☐ sure, sure…	NO ☐ really?
18. Did you enjoy being around your family in your youth?	YES ☐ go to #20	NO ☐ go to #19
19. Did you prefer to be alone in your youth?	YES ☐ go to #21	NO ☐ go to #20
20. Did this change at or around the onset of puberty?	YES ☐ go to #21	NO ☐ go to #23
21. Were you granted the freedom to be alone?	YES ☐ go to #22	NO ☐ go to #23
22. Did you even bother to invent an imaginary friend?	YES ☐ go to # 23	NO ☐ BOOM! E.H.O.!
23. Was your imaginary friend recognized by your family?	YES ☐ go to #24	NO ☐ go to #25
24. Did your imaginary friend prefer to be alone?	YES ☐ BOOM! E.H.O.!	NO ☐ go to #25
25. Did you run away from your imaginary friend?	YES ☐ BOOM! E.H.O.!	NO ☐ yeah, right…

Appendix B
HOW APPROPRIATE IS YOUR RELATIONSHIP WITH YOUR PET?

Yes   No

1) Do you refer to your pet by a nickname even if you named them?

2) Do you feed your pet from the table?

3) Does he sit next to you at the table?

4) Have you fed them a morsal from your own plate?

5) From your mouth?

6) Did you linger after for them to lick any remaining food from your lips?

7) Did that make your legs feel weird?

8) Do you bathe your pet in the shower/bath with you?

9) Are they excused after they're clean?

10) Do you keep them with you until you are done bathing/showering?

11) Have you ever 'dropped the soap'?

12) Does your pet sleep with you and your partner?

13) Has your partner been pushed out of bed by your pet?

14) Has your partner felt passed over by you in favor of your pet?

15) Do you think your pet would make a better partner?

16) Did you replace your partner with your pet?

17) Are you happier now?

Appendix C
GONE BUT NOT FORGOTTEN

INGS FROM
BO
h you were here!

Appendix D
THE LETTERS

To follow in this section is a collection of actual letters written in Phase 4 of our treatment protocol by actual inpatients at our facility. The recipients' names have been redacted to ensure the key protective component of this exercise. This implement is used to unleash the poison of the E.H.O. on those who've contributed to your acquiring it by writing out all your hatefulness and then destroying the account without infecting the one at which it was pointed. In the ceremonial gesture to release the bad feelings associated with this practice, we afford our Overloaders the opportunity to choose any manner with which to befoul their correspondence prior to finally rendering them into the pizza oven and as you will see, some employ great creativity in the process. I hope you enjoy these as much as we do. I think you'll see why this truly *is* my favorite phase of therapy!

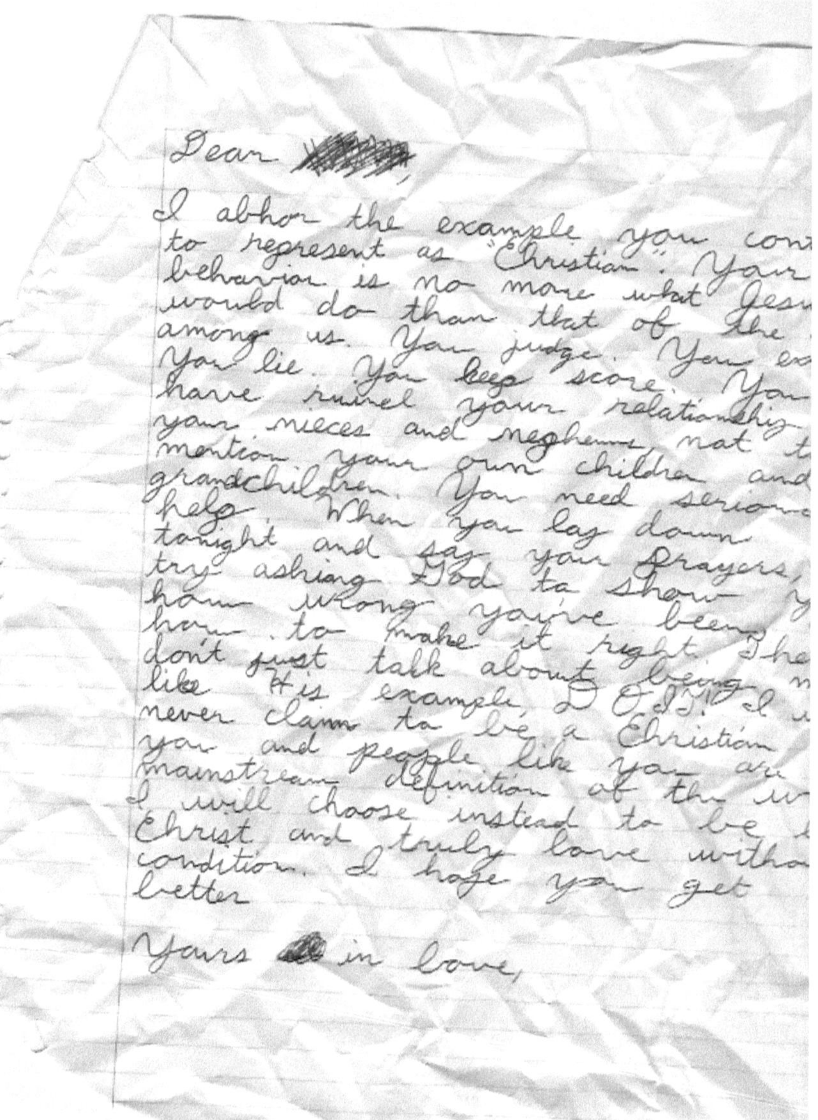

Letter A : Dear [redacted], I abhor the example you continue to represent as "Christian". Your behavior is no more what Jesus would do than that of the worst among us. You judge. You exclude. You lie. You keep score. You have ruined your relationship with your nieces and nephews, not to mention your own children and grandchildren. You need serious help. When you lay down tonight and say your prayers, try asking God to show you how wrong you've been and how to make it right. Then don't just talk about being more like his example, DO IT! I will never claim to be a Christian if you and people like you are the mainstream definition of the word. I will choose instead to be like Christ and truly love without condition. I hope you get better. Yours in love, [redacted]

Hey

I'm sorry I met you. You were clearly <u>NOT</u> the one. You were right about my family though. I just wish you could have seen your own shortcomings as clearly as you could see everyone else's.

Their changing or my changing wasn't up to you. But <u>your</u> changing could have made things completely different. You lost credibility when you projected ALL the blame onto the rest of us.

Anyway... I don't hate you. And I feel bad for hurting you. I hope you can forgive me! And if your friend — the witch — could see to it to vanquish any spell she cast on me, that would be great.

Thanks

Letter B: Hey [redacted], I'm sorry I met you. You were clearly NOT the one. You were right about my family though. I just wish you could have seen your own shortcomings as clearly as you could everyone else's. Their changing or my changing wasn't up to you. But your changing could have made things completely different. You lost credibility when you projected ALL the blame onto the rest of us. Anyway, I don't hate you. And I feel badly for hurting you. I hope you can forgive me. And if your friend the witch could see her way clear to vanquish any spell she cast on me, that would be great. Thanks, [redacted]

Letter C: Dear [redacted], This should not be that hard. You have friends and loved ones that read and know more than you. LISTEN!!!!! Just once in a blue-fucking-moon listen to what someone else has to say and then maybe, just maybe, you won't be such an ignorant asshole! Yours truly, [redacted]

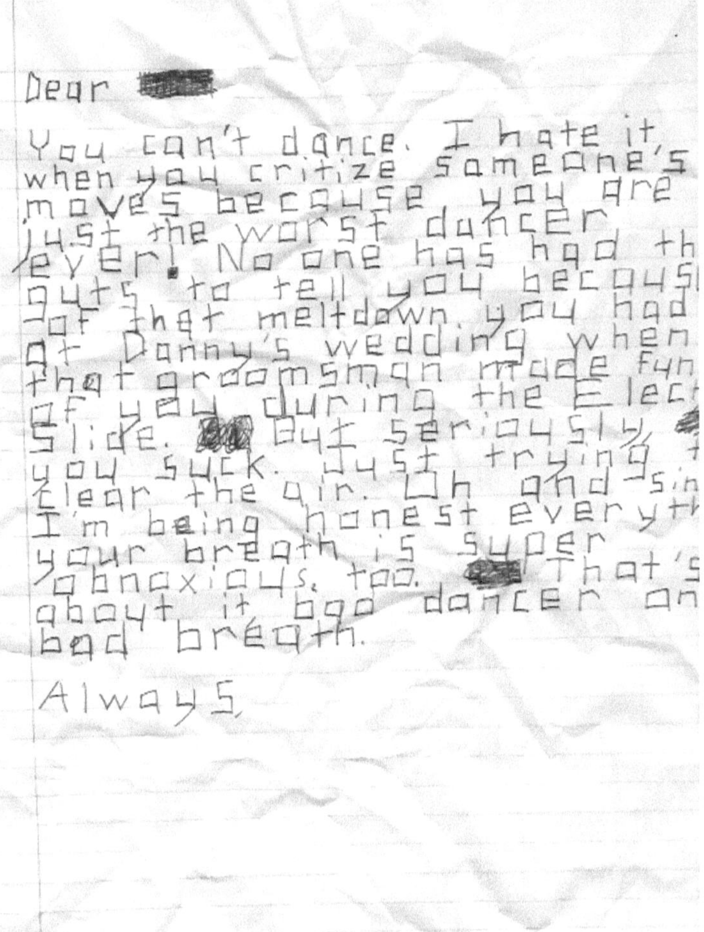

Letter D: Dear [redacted], You can't dance. I hate it when you criticize someone's moves because you are just the worst dancer ever! No one has had the guts to tell you because of that meltdown you had at Danny's wedding when that groomsman made fun of you during the Electric Slide. But seriously, _____, you suck. Just trying to clear the air. Oh and since I'm being honest and everything, you breath is super obnoxious too. That's about it, bad dancer and bad breath. Always, [redacted]

I FIND IT ALMOST IMPOSSIBLE to tolerate your increasing whining. Your inability to complete even the most Elementary ~~tasks~~ in life makes it hard to even feel sorry for you. Stop your ungodly whining + blaming everyone else for your mistakes + lack of direction in your life. You have no one to blame but yourself for your MISERABLE EXISTENCE (and you have the power to change your life if _YOU_ want to) so if you don't want a happy life — don't bother including me in your circle + will help in "your circle yours. xo

Letter E: Dear [redacted], I find it almost impossible to tolerate your incessant whining. Your inability to complete even the most elementary tasks in life makes it hard to even feel sorry for you. Stop your ungodly whining and blaming everyone else for your mistakes and pick a direction for your life. You have no one to blame but yourself for your miserable existence and you have the power to change your life if you want to. So if you don't want a happy full life, don't bother including me in your circle. If you do want to be productive and enjoy life, get on with it and call me when you get on with it. Yours truly, [redacted]

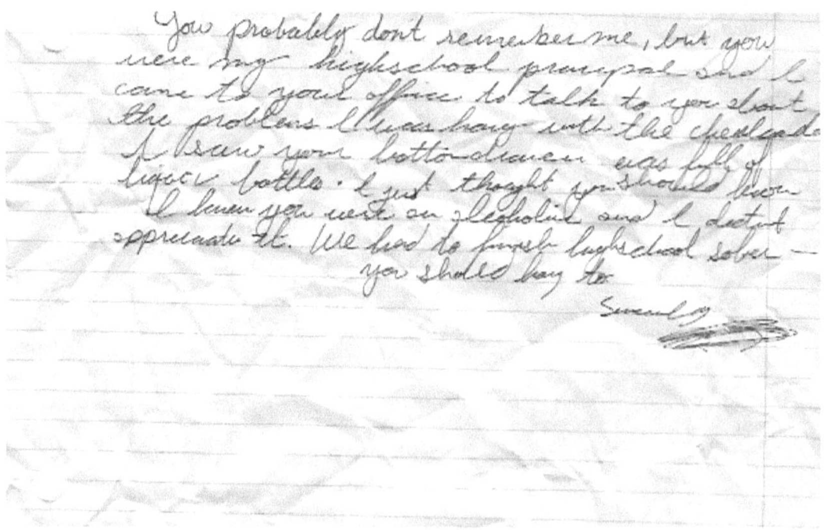

Letter F: Dear [redacted], You probably don't remember this but when you were my high school principal and I came to your office to talk to you about the problems I was having with the cheerleaders, I saw your bottom drawer was full of liquor bottles. I just thought you should know I knew you were an alcoholic. And I didn't appreciate it. We had to face high school sober, you should have too. Sincerely, [redacted]

i hated the way you used to
SCOWL
at me and my brother when we came to ur store.
(Just so you know — of all the kids that hung out there, we were the only two who DIDN'T steal anything.

He is dead now, but if he were here he would want you to know that neither of us deserved the dirty looks u gave us. And he would also prolly tell u that it was me who set fire to ur wife car for looking at us the way u did.

p.s. Sorry about ur cat
I didn't know she was in the back seat

Letter G: [redacted] I hated the way you used to scowl at me when my brother and I came into your store. Just so you know, of all the kids we hung out with, [redacted]and I were the only two guys that didn't steal anything from you. [redacted]'s dead now, but if he were here I know he would want you to know that neither of us deserved the dirty looks you gave us. And he would also probably tell you that it was me who set fire to your wife's car for looking at us the way you did. Sorry about your cat. I didn't know she was in the back seat. Truly, [redacted]

Letter H: My Dear [redacted], I hope this letter finds you well. Please take a note that I quit hanging out with you because you are a bigot and a pig and I cannot tolerate your behavior another minute. I hope you fall on something sharp. Give my best to your mom. I miss her cabbage rolls. I must get her recipe. All the best, [redacted]

Appendix E

Jerome and Goldie 4eva

Nora the Narwhal and her Curly Horn
by Alan Maynard, Illustrated by Soma Cather

Mumblings: West Virginia Horror Stories by Caitlyn Pace

Afterwords by Stephen Bias

The Dictionary Game by Mike Hornyak

About the Author

Diana Johnson, who's contemporary fiction titles include Cold Daughters, Just DIY, and The Value of Miss M, resides in Bridgeport, WV. Non-Dr. Deidre Johnston resides in Diana Johnson's imagination and continuously looks for logical ways for people to navigate these illogical times. Visit dianajohnsonwriter.com for insight into and connection with both.

Notes